CHARLOTTE'S STORY

GLORIA OKOSI

UrbanPress
PUBLISHING YOUR DREAMS

Charlotte's Story
by Gloria Okosi
Copyright ©2025 Gloria Okosi

ISBN 978-1-63360-332-5

For Worldwide Distribution
Printed in the U.S.A.

Urban Press
PO Box 5044
Williamsburg, VA 23188
757.808.5776
www.urbanpress.us

This book is dedicated to my children:
Ore Okosi, Felicia Linch, and Frances Okosi;

and my grandchildren:
Obiora, Abigail, Melody, and Jonathan Okosi.

A special thanks to Frances for her help and
encouragement in completing the book.

CHAPTER 1

FIVE MINUTES MORE

It was a hot sunny day in June and Charlotte had been off school on a revision day as she prepared to sit for her CXC exams. She had taken a book and sat under the large mahogany tree near her home. It was a familiar spot where children often hung out as they swung from the low hanging branches of the tree or sat on the ground to play Jacks and Pickup. Charlotte could hear the shouts of boys playing cricket in the open pasture nearby as the sun was heading towards the horizon. As she caught the passing breeze that blew across from the palm trees on the hill above the house, she drifted off to sleep.

When Charlotte awoke, she knew it would soon be time to head back to the house to complete the chores her Aunt Maisie had left her to do, but she thought she would give herself five minutes more and read another chapter of the book. As she began to read once again, she heard the shouts of the boys:

"Come on, Albert," came the shouts from Melvin, "hit him for six. Run, run Albert, run."

"Four runs" shouted another voice, "you bowling bare sweet water."

Joe came down the hill to where the boys were playing. "Want a game, Joe?" Melvin aked.

"Alright, but I have got to go home and change out of my school clothes. I'll be back in five minutes."

"We don't have time for that, Joe. You either want to play now or you can forget it."

Joe reluctantly threw down his homemade cotton school bag and took up his position as a fielder behind the batsman. As Joe stood there, he knew full well that if a mark or spot of tar from the newly made rag and tar ball got on his uniform, he would be in for a thrashing or worse - he would have to go to bed without any supper as his punishment. Joe imagined his mother's voice as he leaped to catch the ball, "Where you been all this time boy? School finished ages ago."

"Nowhere, Ma," he would say.

"Don't lie to me, boy. How that tar got on them brand new trousers?"

Joe's mind went back to the game. If he was careful, Ma wouldn't find out that he didn't come straight home from school, so he continued to play. Usually he was a good fielder and not many balls went past him without being caught and the batsman being stumped, but today he wasn't focused.

A short while after the game started (though to Joe who was distracted, it seemed like forever), the boys saw Millicent coming along the dirt track. Millicent was a young woman but with the mental age of a ten-year-old. She was also deaf.

Although the adults in the neighbourhood understood Millicent, the children often didn't and so they made fun of her. Joe knew that this was the one time he dared not join the other children in teasing Millicent because she lived next door to him. Just as one of the boys, Clifford, was about to call out to Millicent, Joe slammed the palm of his hand across the boy's mouth,

"Don't do that! You want her to tell Ma she saw me playing cricket?"

The two boys walked a few steps towards Millicent with Clifford's hand now around Joe's shoulders.

"I tell you what we'll do, man," said Clifford. "Let's talk to her nicely and ask her if she wants help to take the load of goat grass she's carrying home. She's bound to like that."

"You think so, Cliff? Okay, I'll talk to her nicely."

"Hi, Millie, can I help you with the grass?"

Millicent looked around her. *Surely this boy could not be speaking to me*, she thought. She was so accustomed to being teased by the neighbourhood children that she wasn't sure what to do. Joe gestured with his hands, pointing to the grass and then to his head with a big smile on his face. Millicent slowly lowered the grass from her head and handed it to Joe.

"See you, Cliff," Cliff winked at Joe as he left.

Millicent and Joe walked along the track together until Joe got to the entrance of his house, where he rested the grass he'd been carrying on the ground and said goodbye to Millicent.

With a sudden jolt, Charlotte jumped to her feet, the book falling to the ground. She had drifted back to sleep yet again. *Goodness me,* she thought, *how long have I been asleep?* It was then that Charlotte realised she had been dreaming. The dream had taken her back to the time when she was cared for by her grandmother and would play cricket with her cousin, Marcia, and the other children in the neighbourhood. This was a pastime which Aunt Maisie frowned upon as she considered it to be a waste of time and not a game for girls. Back in those days, the girls would only ever be allowed to be fielders while the boys got to bat.

Hoping she would have enough time to to complete her chores before Aunt Maisie got home, she hurried back to the house.

CHAPTER 2

MEMORIES OF MOTHER AND GRANDMOTHER

To Charlotte's surprise, her aunt Maisie and cousins Charlie, Marcia, and Yvonne, had already reached home by the time she got back and her aunt had started the evening meal.

Charlotte could feel her heart pounding as she walked into the house. She was expecting a scolding and berating from her aunt. This had become the normal pattern of her aunt's attitude towards Charlotte since the passing of Charlotte's grandmother. Her aunt seemed to take every opportunity to scold and belittle Charlotte, and would often remind her she was no longer the "princess" she thought she was, and she should be glad to have a roof over her head. Her Aunt Maisie considered her spoilt and useless and often told

Charlotte that she was like her mother who had abandoned her.

In the months since her grandmother's death, Charlotte often felt lost and lonely. Letters from her mother were infrequent and seemed emotionally distant. Her only other connections to her mother were photographs and the memory she had of her on the day she left the Island, when Charlotte and her grandmother had gone with her mother to the harbour where she was to board the large ship taking her to England.

Charlotte could still remember the feeling she had as a four-year old, of being frightened and sick inside. She had cried when her mother hugged her goodbye at the harbour dock. But her grandmother had held Charlotte tightly and promised her that she would be okay and that she would see her mother again soon when she sent for her to come to England.

Charlotte and her grandmother had boarded the bus home, and five minutes later they reached the house. Her grandmother told her if she sat on the rock on the hill above the house, she would see the boat as it left the harbour. As Charlotte turned to go up the hill, her grandmother told her she too would come out to see the boat leave. Charlotte raced up the hill where she could see the boat in the far distance. She could hear the honking that came from the boat indicating it was about to leave the harbour. Her grandmother came up to her on the hill bringing her a red ice lolly. Charlotte was delighted and immediately started to lick the lolly as she dangled her feet over the edge of the rock.

She and grandmother sat on the rock and

watched the boat as it went over the blue horizon out of sight. That night Charlotte slept snuggled closely beside her grandmother, and she promised Charlotte that if she was a good little girl, she would buy her her own bed and place it right next to hers. Charotte's grandmother taught her to say her prayers at night kneeling beside the bed. She told her to always remember that God was a good father and she should always thank him at the end of the day for watching over her and keeping her safe. It took her grandmother a while to help Charlotte understand God being a father. Charlotte had wanted to know if her grandmother meant God was her godfather, just like how Aunt Sylvia was her godmother.

Charlotte often thought of the day of her grandmother's funeral, her body laying in the coffin at the front of the church. The organ had played as the mourners sang along to the hymn "Abide with me, fast fall the eventide" and Charlotte had wondered why she had never heard that hymn sung except at funerals, or when Aunt Maisie and her grandmother had an argument. The hymn, and the feeling of sadness, had taken her back to the day she said goodbye to her mother at the docks whilst holding on to the huge dry hand of her grandmother.

Charlotte was still finding it difficult to come to terms with the loss of her grandmother. She had written to her mother to ask if she had made any plans for Charlotte to join her in the UK, but as yet no plans had been made.

Charlotte remembered how, on the day of the funeral, she sat quietly in the church next to her cousin Charlie, and as the service was about to close, the family were invited to take one last look at her grandmother. They told them that in five minutes she would be taken to her final resting place. Charlotte could not bring herself to move, but then she suddenly felt someone tugging at her sleeve, prompting her to move. Charlotte knew that of all the people who should have taken one last look at her grandmother it should have been her, but she could not bring herself to see her beloved granny in the coffin.

Charlotte rose to her feet and walked quickly to the back door of the church where she stood and waited outside. She knew that once she got home she would have to answer to her aunt and other members of the family for not joining them as they gathered around the coffin in the church. She knew she would be labelled an ungrateful child and would be told once again that she was like her thoughtless mother who had abandoned her in pursuit of her own happiness.

Charlotte remembered how she had stood at the graveside not knowing what to do. All she could think of then was the prayer her grandmother had taught her and so she prayed, "Now I lay me down to sleep, I pray the Lord my soul to keep. If I should die before I wake, I pray the Lord my soul to take." Charlotte thought of the many times she had heard her grandmother and others repeat the words of the preacher on the radio who encouraged them during times of sadness or distress to remember, "Weeping may tarry for the night, but joy comes in the morning."

On the way home sitting in the car next to her cousin Charlie, Charlotte wondered what would become of her now that her grandmother had gone. Charlie had always been kind to her and treated her like she was his sister. Although he was only two years older than Charlotte, he would always defend Charlotte against his mother's sharp tongue. Charlotte thought of the number of arguments between her aunt and grandmother. They were mostly about Charlotte as her aunt always considered her spoilt and, as she would say, "full of herself." Her aunt had hated that her grandmother protected her and had seemed to lavish every penny of her pension on Charlotte. She was always one of the best-dressed children at church and her uniforms were always immaculately taken care of by her grandmother, even though Charlotte was old enough to take care of them herself.

As they reached home, some of the mourners had already arrived back at the house for the repast. It made Charlotte cross to see people tucking into food and drinks and seeming to be so happy when inside her own heart was breaking. She wondered how it was possible that people who had wept so hard at the graveside only moments before were able to talk and laugh as though everything was back to normal. Charlotte sat in the front room watching the people who talked, laughed, and drank. Charlotte then saw her aunt moving towards her and felt sure this was the moment her aunt would humiliate her in front of all the people. It would be about her not taking a last look at her grandmother in the church. But instead, Aunt Maisie shouted at her, "Girl, leave this room at once! What are you sitting there for? Get to the kitchen and help with the washing up."

In the kitchen, her cousin Marcia was washing the dishes. Charlotte offered to take over, but

Marcia told her she could do the drying. Charlotte could see that Marcia had been crying. There was a long silence between the girls before Marcia spoke. She told Charlotte that she had overheard her mother saying that now that their grandmother had gone, Charlotte would have to stop being so "puffed up and be like everyone else." She might even have to stop going to high school and go to work. Charlotte had not even had time to think so far ahead. She had never imagined being without her grandmother.

She suddenly thought, *Could Marcia be right? Had Aunt Maisie made those plans already?* Charlotte consoled herself into thinking that Marcia must have been mistaken, as she often was, since Marcia was in the habit of earwigging and prying around corners. But Charlotte couldn't shake the thought. *If she had to stop school and go to work, what kind of work could she even do?* Charlotte decided that she would do what her grandmother had always taught her, and she heard her voice saying, "Worry about things when the time comes."

Later when everyone had gone and all the family was ready for bed, Charlotte was a bit apprehensive about going to bed. Since her mother had left for England, Charlotte had shared a tiny bedroom with her grandmother. The room held two single beds, a trunk, a plastic hanging wardrobe, a mirror, and a picture with Jesus and his disciples at the Last Supper. Charlotte looked around the room as if seeing it for the first time. As her eyes rested on the bed where only a few days ago her grandmother's body laid until they took her to the funeral home, she remembered all the duppy stories she had ever heard and she could not bring herself to touch the bed. Charlotte wanted to throw herself on the bed and weep like she did when she was a young child, when her grandmother would wrap her arms around her and reassure her it would all be okay. Charlotte had not wanted to spend the night in the room alone, but she knew her aunt would insist she do so, and be in the dark as punishment.

Suddenly the door swung open. Charlotte jumped to her feet holding her hands to her chest. Aunt Maisie stood at the door with Marcia following closely behind her. "From now on you will be sharing this room with Marcia. Marcia can have your bed and you can have my mother's bed."

Charlotte began to cry, "But this is my bed. I've always slept in this bed."

Her aunt replied gruffly, "Never mind that. No arguments! Put out the light and do as you are told. You ought to be glad for a roof over your head. From now on, things are going to be different around here."

Charlotte consoled herself with the fact that at least she would not have to spend the night in the dark room alone. Besides, her grandmother loved her and so her ghost would not return to frighten her. She remembered too that one of their relatives had already spent last night in grandmother's bed whilst her body had been at the funeral home.

Slowly Charlotte got into her nightdress and crept into the bed. Neither she nor Marcia spoke a word. She knew that Marcia was just as afraid as she was. All the lamps in the house were beginning to go out one by one. As the house went silent, Charlotte pulled the sheet as far over her head as it would go.

"Good night, Marcia."

When Marcia did not respond Charlotte knew that Marcia was asleep. Charlotte tried not to think of her grandmother's lifeless body lying in the cemetery. She began to whisper the prayer "Now I lay me down to sleep . . ."

Charlotte awoke to the sound of a voice yelling at her to get up. Yawning and stretching she mumbled, "Five minutes more, Granny, just give me five minutes more."

"How much longer you two are going to stay in there?"

It was then Charlotte realised it was not her grandmother calling her to get up but her Aunt Maisie.

"Come on, shift yourselves and come and help Charlie to collect the water before the water go off and before anybody leaves this house."

Pointing at Charlotte she said, "And you, Madam, can get started on cleaning up the kitchen."

Charlotte drew herself to the side of the bed. She gathered her clothes and prepared to head to the shower. Whilst in the shower she wondered what the day, and the rest of her life, had in store for her. How would she get by without her be-loved grandmother? She felt tears beginning to fill her eyes. She didn't think anyone would ever be as good to her as her grandmother had been.

CHAPTER 3

AUNT MAISIE AND COUSIN MARCIA

A year had passed since her grandmother's death and, while Charlotte still felt the pain of losing her, she was coming to terms with the loss. She had even begun to sense some mellowing in Aunt Maisie's attitude towards her. So much so that on her sixteenth birthday, when Charlotte had received a birthday card as usual from her mother enclosing a postal order for ten pounds, Aunt Masie had allowed Charlotte to take the money to the post office to be changed into local currency. She even told Charlotte she could spend $5 of the money, but to be sure not to spend it on rubbish!

Up to that point, Aunt Maisie had made no mention of her stopping school and going to work. Charlotte felt sure that Marcia had been wrong all along. Charlotte did wonder at times why Aunt Maisie had allowed her to continue going to high school whilst her own daughter had already left school and was attending sewing classes. After all, Marcia was just as smart as Charlotte, if not smarter. Charlotte also wondered where the money for her school fees was coming from. She knew the money her mother sent was infrequent and very little and she suspected that her grandmother had been using her pension to pay her school fees.

Charlotte also thought that her aunt allowing her to continue to go to school might be due to her appearance. She realised long ago that people like Charlotte, with very pale complexion and soft curly hair, were given preferential treatment and privileges above others with darker skins, even though they were secretly whispered about and called names.

Since the death of their grandmother, Charlotte and Marcia had grown closer. They shared teenage secrets and giggled as many teenagers do. Yvonne, Aunt Maisie's youngest daughter and the youngest in the household, often felt left out and would plead with the older girls to take her with them. She would hang around Charlotte calling her "Lottie." Charlotte hated to be called Lottie. She had only ever accepted being called Lottie by her grandmother and her cousin Charlie. Charlie was now eighteen years old and he had little time for the younger children. Marcia felt quite grown up, being fifteen years old and no longer at school. She too had little time for Yvonne and would insist she go away and find friends her own age.

One afternoon, Charlotte arrived home

from school to find Aunt Maisie sitting in the front room. She beckoned Charlotte to come and sit with her as they needed to talk. As Charlotte sat down, her aunt immediately demanded to know what nonsense she had been writing to her mother.

"How could you show such ingratitude by lying about the way you're being treated, after all I have been doing to keep you in school, and to clothe and feed you."

Charlotte was shocked, but before she could respond, her aunt produced a letter and handed it to Charlotte. It was her mother's reply to a letter Charlotte had written in which she had expressed her longing to be with her mother and begged her to bring her to England and take her away from this place. Charlotte had been waiting for weeks for the reply—and finally her mother had written, asking why Charlotte was so unhappy living with Aunt Maisie and anxious to leave. Her aunt had opened the letter and read it and clearly misunderstood every line of its content. Charlotte sobbed as she tried to explain what she had written in the letter to her mother but her explanation was not accepted.

"You will never write another word to your mother before showing me what you've written!"

On Sunday Charlotte and Marcia went to Sunday School as normal. Charlotte was still hurting after the conversation with her aunt but tried to carry on as though nothing had happened. When they returned from service Marcia seemed excited. She turned to Charlotte and said, "I need your help."

"With what?" Charlotte replied.

Marcia then told Charlotte that she wanted to go to church that evening for choir practice. She asked Charlotte if she'd come with her, and back her up when she told her mother they were to meet with other churches in the city to practice for an upcoming joint program. Charlotte wanted to know why Marcia wanted to go to church in the city and refused to back up Marcia's story without knowing all the facts.

Marcia asked, "Can you keep a secret?"

Charlotte replied, "That depends."

Marcia told Charlotte she was seeing a boy called Brian and had arranged to meet him at the city's bus stand.

"You stupid or what? Of all the places you could meet. The bus stand? Don't you know that someone who knows your mother could see you and tell her?"

Marcia pressed on, explaining her plan and suggesting that they could leave the house together at the same time, but that she would skip church and meet Brian. They would then meet up again at the end of the service and return home together. Charlotte was unhappy with the plan but as she and Marcia had become very close, she did not want to be on bad terms with her. So she agreed, but pleaded with Marcia to be careful.

For several weeks after that the meetings between Marcia and Brian continued. Charlotte was becoming tired of deceiving her aunt and so she told Marcia it was time she either stopped meeting with Brian in the city or she would tell her aunt. When Marcia did finally decide to tell her mother she was seeing Brian, the response could not have been any easier. Aunt Maisie agreed without any hesitation and commended Marcia for her open-ness and honesty and commented that Charlotte should take a leaf from Marcia's book.

CHAPTER 4

CHARLOTTE'S FUTURE

Charlotte sat at the table surrounded by books as she read by the glow of the small oil lamp. She was struggling to concentrate because of the noise and music coming from the radio in the corner of the front room and the chatter from the other members of the family. Although Charlotte was preparing for her CXC exams, Aunt Maisie had insisted the lamps in the house must be out by 9 p.m. to save oil. It was too dark in the early morning hours to see by natural light so each evening as soon as she could after her meal and her chores, Charlotte settled down to her revision.

Two weeks before Charlotte was about to take her first exam, Aunt Maisie informed her that at the end of the month she would no longer be able to go to high school. The school fees were too much. "And besides," she had said, "your support stopped on your sixteenth birthday."

Charlotte was stunned. What support? She didn't understand. Since her grandmother's death, no one had mentioned school fees—everything regarding school had continued as usual. Charlotte knew that her mother was still unable to send very much money from England. And since Charlotte's letter to her mother about her future had not yielded a reply, she never raised the issue again. Charlotte was too afraid to ask her aunt what exactly she meant about the "support."

Aunt Maisie told Charlotte that she would have to find a job. Charlotte had been looking forward to sitting for her exams the following month. She felt sure she was going to do well as she had dedicated herself to studying and had dreamed of doing well enough in the exams to allow her to apply to a college in the UK, in the hopes of joining her mother. Whatever was she to do now? Where was she to look for work and what work could she do? She knew of girls who had worked at Woollies and the Five-and-Ten store, so perhaps she could find similar work there, or even at the ice cream parlour.

Charlotte hadn't thought of her grandmother in weeks, but suddenly she loomed large as life before her. She wanted to throw herself into her grandmother's arms as she did as a child. Tears rolled down Charlotte's cheeks as she listened to her aunt without really making sense of what she was saying. She folded her books away and wondered if there was any point in continuing to study until the end of the month or even taking the exams.

As Charlotte went to bed, thoughts flooded her mind. If she had to leave school and possibly work in an ice cream parlour, she would be humiliated by some of the children from her school. They already thought her "stuck up and full of herself." That thought chilled her to the bone, so she decided that in the morning she would tell her aunt she would go to the city to look for a job.

Charlotte rose early in the morning bracing herself to discuss her plan with Aunt Maisie. No sooner had she voiced what her intentions were she was scolded and told she was being "uppish." Aunt Maisie told her she was to continue school until she was told to stop.

Undaunted by her aunt's reaction, Charlotte held on to the plan she had in mind. She left for school at the usual time and on her way she started firming up her plan. She knew she could not go into a store looking for work dressed in her school uniform. So she decided to wait until Saturday morning when she was due to return her books to the library. She would pay particular attention to the way she dressed, especially her hair (which she believed was her best feature) and use it to her advantage. But she had to be careful not to arouse suspicion with Aunt Maisie.

After school that day, Charlotte walked into the Five-and-Ten store. From the money she had left from her mother's postal order, Charlotte bought herself a cheap red lipstick, a large circle comb, and a large pair of earrings. She would keep these hidden in her school bag.

As Charlotte walked home, she continued her planning. On Saturday morning she would dress as normal to go to the library and leave at the usual time. But when out of sight, she would pile her long, curly hair high on her head, and wear her large, hooped earrings and the red lipstick. The image warmed her inside and she began to lose the fear of having to face the world as an adult.

On Saturday morning, Charlotte prepared to leave the house for the library just as she'd planned. She wanted to get it over with as quickly as possible. She did not like the idea of deceiving her aunt, and she remembered how awful she had felt when she covered for Marcia with Brian. But this was important and was for her future, so she just had to disregard her feelings.

After she got off the bus outside the library, she quickly went inside and handed in her books. She then made her way quickly to the ladies room where she piled her hair up in a ponytail high on her head. She applied the red lipstick and put in her earrings and removed her socks. She took a long look at herself. She was satisfied with the way she looked. *Surely someone would hire me*, she thought. She didn't have time to waste. She needed to hurry as she wanted to check several stores for vacancies. She also had to return to the library to redress herself and be home in time without making Aunt Maisie cross, or suspicious.

The first three stores Charlotte enquired at turned her down. They were already over-staffed and she was advised to try again in a few weeks as the school holidays were approaching. In one of the back streets in town there were several one-door Indian-owned stores which could only afford one assistant at a time. *If I can get a job at one of those stores, it would be a start*, Charlotte thought to herself. As she entered the first of these stores she could feel her heart pounding. The store seemed to be stocked with all manner of merchandise and leaning on the counter was a man she presumed to be the owner. Charlotte did not know what to say as she approached him but thankfully he spoke up first.

"Hello, can I help you? Want cloth to make dress?"

"No, no thank you," she stammered. "I'm looking for work. I wonder if you might be needing someone to work during the week or even only on Saturdays?"

The man looked her up and down. Charlotte avoided making any eye contact but instead focused on the items around the store. She felt like running out of the store when suddenly the man walked behind her and said "You ever worked in a store before?"

Charlotte thought quickly "Yes, I work in a store now but it will be closing down in two weeks. I'm on my lunch break so I thought I would make a few inquiries to find something new before it closes."

"How old are you, eighteen? How far you live?"

"Just outside the city. I come to work by bus. It only takes twenty minutes into the city."

The man explained he needed an assistant but had to consult with his brother first. He suggested she come back around five in the evening after the store closed. *Five,* thought Charlotte. She could not come back to the city at five or wait around until then. What would she tell Aunt Maisie? She said "If you give me the phone number, I'll call you or I can come back in next Saturday," thinking that by then he would have spoken to his brother and would know for sure if he needed someone.

The man agreed, and gave her the number. "Thank you. Got to get back to work" she said, as she hurriedly left the store.

Charlotte began to head towards the bus stop when she remembered she had to return to the library to change. She ran all the way and reached the library with barely enough time before it closed to remove the lipstick and earrings, re-do her hair and put on her socks. She collected two books. She couldn't tell Aunt Maisie she'd been to the library and return empty-handed. As she got to the librarian with the books, she was told she could only take out one fiction and she had better hurry up if she wanted to choose another as she only had five minutes. Charlotte did not particularly care what the books were, she just wanted to get two books and be on her way home, so she ran to the nearest shelf and picked a book. She glared at the librarian as she slammed the selection of books down and waited for them to be stamped. Finally, she was able to leave.

Sunday passed in the usual quiet way. All the members of the family attended morning service, except for Charlie, who considered himself too grown-up to attend church, and Aunt Maisie, who stayed behind to cook the Sunday lunch.

As the family gathered to eat lunch, Aunt Maisie announced that she had at last found a job for Charlotte, it was to be the assistant cook at the Big House, the plantation house owned by the Evans family. Shocked by the announcement,

Charlotte held her fork between her mouth and her plate unable to comprehend what her aunt was saying. The other members of the family likewise sat wide-eyed and dumbfounded. Charlotte could feel tears beginning to form in her eyes but managed to contain them. She replied to her aunt that she had seen an advert in the library for a shop assistant in a store in the city. On passing the store, she had enquired about the job and was told to come back next week to follow up on the vacancy. Immediately Aunt Maisie wanted to know all about the job, where it was, who owned the store, how much it was paying. Charlotte did not have any of these details so she told her aunt she was asked by the owner to call back. She promised Aunt Maisie to have all the answers by the weekend.

As always Charlie was on hand to back Charlotte up. He was not going to let his mother bully Charlotte into working in the Evans' kitchen, especially as he had heard rumours about his family and the Evans. Charlie had heard these rumours through his girlfriend who said they had surfaced just before Charlotte was born. Charlie had decided to keep all he had heard to himself, but he wondered why his mother would want Charlotte to work at the Evans's since she must know the rumours too. He thought it was best to try his hardest to persuade his mother to change her mind about sending Charlotte to work at the Big House.

Later, as Marcia and Charlotte made their way to evening service, Marcia's friend Cindy joined them. As they walked, Charlotte was quieter than usual and Cindy asked, "Is everything okay?"

Marcia proceeded to relate the story of Charlotte having to leave school and to go to work and how she was feeling a bit upset. Upon hearing this, Cindy laughed and said, "Why should she feel upset? She got Island Passport."

Both Cindy and Marcia giggled. Charlotte looked at them and wanted to know what they meant as she did not yet have any kind of passport. Marcia laughed again and explained to Charlotte that it meant that people of light complexion had an advantage because their colour could get them anywhere. This made Charlotte even more upset as any reference to the pale colour of her skin always made her feel uneasy and an outcast from any of their friends.

As the girls returned home from church, Charlotte told Marcia that she was not happy that Marcia had shared with Cindy that Charlotte might be having to leave school and go to work when she had not properly processed the idea herself. Marcia laughed it off, saying it wasn't a big deal.

As agreed, Charlotte decided to follow up on the phone call to the store in the city. To her dismay, she was told the position had been taken but she could try again nearer to the Christmas holidays. She said thank you and hung up. What would she do now? She had already tried most of the stores in the city. She had no other choice but to explore the ice cream parlours. It would be better than working in the Evans' kitchen. But how would she break the news to her aunt that she was not successful with the job in the city? Now she'd have no way of countering her aunt's plan. Charlotte's heart was heavy. She had no doubt her aunt would be pleased to hear the news and would see it as bringing Charlotte "down a peg or two."

The girls prepared themselves to go to bed. Little Yvonne was already asleep, Charlie was still out, and Aunt Maisie would not go to bed until Charlie was back home. Not long after the girls went to bed, they heard raised voices. It was Aunt Maisie and Charlie. They wondered what the noise was about but dared not leave their beds to find out. Besides, Aunt Maisie was sure to tell them it was none of their business. However, Marcia always had her way of snooping. She crept to the bedroom door and, leaving it slightly open, she stood behind the door to listen, beckoning Charlotte to join her. Reluctantly, Charlotte left her bed and stood behind Marcia. Charlotte whispered, "Charlie must be getting a telling off for coming in late."

Marcia whispered back, "Charlie never gets told off for coming home late. The argument is about you."

"Why would it be about me?" Charlotte whispered.

"Listen, listen," Marcia said.

Charlotte could only hear her name but could not hear clearly as both voices spoke at the same time. Marcia heard perfectly as she was accustomed to listening through keyholes. She told Charlotte,

"Charlie is saying to Mama that he would see to it that on no account you were going to work in the Evans' kitchen. And Mama said if Charlie thinks he is the man of this house, she would see about that."

The girls heard a door slam and all went

quiet. Marcia and Charlotte crept back into bed and said goodnight to each other. Charlotte laid awake for what seemed like hours trying to figure out her future.

CHAPTER 5

PA EVANS AND THE BIG HOUSE

Monday morning began with its usual frenzy. Aunt Maisie was getting ready for work whilst issuing orders about the chores she expected done by the time she got home in the evening. Charlie was rushing through the door to catch the first bus to the 'country,' a parish some distance from the city and their home. Charlie had been working as an apprentice carpenter since he finished school and having completed his apprenticeship, he was working with a contractor on a large building project. That meant he left early for work in the morning and returned home late in the evenings.

Charlie was now nearly nineteen years old. He was not expected to do chores but would on occasions help with any odd jobs around the house that were considered "man's work." Marcia and Charlotte, on the other hand, had found that their chores had increased now they were getting older. There was the cleaning of the house, ironing (though they were not trusted with all items of clothing), collecting water each morning if the mains water went off, and of course, their biggest job was taking care of Yvonne. They dressed her, combed and plaited her hair, made her lunch along with their own, and dropped her off at the school gate before they made their own way to school and sewing classes.

Charlotte arrived at school in a very low mood and this Monday morning felt like no other. She wasn't sure but she felt she was getting side glances from other girls in the class. She wondered if Cindy had already spread the word that she might be having to leave school and go to work, possibly as a cook in the Evans' household. She found it hard to concentrate in class that morning, although the topic was English, her best subject. Charlotte could not wait for the day to end. She was hoping that by the time she reached home Marcia would have found out more about the argument between her mother and Charlie. She hoped that her aunt would relent.

Marcia and Aunt Maisie often reached home before Charlotte who had to wait for the bus from the city. Although the journey was not long the buses ran infrequently. Charlotte knew that Marcia had a clever way of getting around her mother and finding out things that were sometimes only meant for grown-ups to know about. Perhaps by the time she reached home, Marcia would have some news for her that would lift the sullen mood she had felt all day.

To her surprise when she arrived home Charlie was already home. Charlotte greeted Charlie with half a smile and said, "You're home early, how come?"

Charlie smiled back, "That's for me to know and you to find out."

As the family sat down to the evening meal Aunt Maisie had prepared, Charlie announced that he had something he wanted to tell the family. He first began by apologising to his mother for the way he spoke to her last night. He then went on to say, "I went to work today just to let my boss know I needed the day off as I had something to do."

Everyone was wondering what Charlie had to do. He went on. "I needed the day off because I went to the Big House to see old man Evans."

At this, Aunt Maisie rolled her eyes and shouted, "What on earth you think you were doing going to see Mr Evans? I told you last night, our problems are nobody's business but ours, and especially not the business of Mr. Evans. Besides, what's it got to do with the matter at hand?"

Charlie said, "He owes this family a favour and it was about time we call it in."

Mr. Evans was the owner of the plantation at the bottom of the hill where Charlotte and her family lived. He had become the new owner of the plantation when the white plantation owners sold out and returned to England. Charlotte knew that her grandmother often visited the Big House and had a very good relationship with the Evans, but as far as Charlotte knew, they never employed her grandmother at the Big House

Charlotte's mother and grandmother had sometimes spoken of the Evans family. On occasions when there was a party at the Big House when every room in the house appeared to be lit up, the light would spill over onto the driveway, and it would seem like millions of cars and people were going into the Big House.

Years later as Charlotte got older, she remembered her aunt and some of the people who stood outside her window gossiping at night talking of the lavish parties that went on at the Big House. One woman said that when the Evans moved into the Big House, drinks flowed like water and the food was "out of this world." She had said that the boss had seen the kind of food and drink the members of his club and lodge consumed and he had left nothing lacking.

Aunt Maisie and the local women cried shame at the fate of the owners. Within a few short years of taking ownership of the plantation, the mistress had passed away from a long-standing condition and Mr. Evans lived with his son, his daughter-in-law, and their two children.

As the women gossiped, Aunt Maisie would deliver one of her famous sayings like, "Wa in catch ya in pass ya," meaning, "just because you haven't yet suffered a particular fate, doesn't mean you've escaped it." She never needed to explain to her listener what she meant as they knew the familiar sayings and attached their own meaning to them.

Once or twice, Mr. Evans had given Charlotte a ride to school and had enquired of her mother. He had told Charlotte that her grandmother should be very proud of her mum—she had done a good job of bringing her up.

Charlie continued recounting his story. As Charlie arrived at the Big House, he was shown into Mr. Evans' study. As they met, Charlie introduced himself as Charles Brown, grandson of Ivy Beckles and nephew of Amanda Beckles.

Mr. Evans said, "I know who you are, boy."

Immediately, Charlie had corrected him, "Don't call me 'boy,' Boss. My name is Charles Brown. Most people call me Charlie."

Inside, Charlie was seething with anger that someone like Mr. Evans, who, as a descendent of former white indentured labourers, who would himself likely have suffered the indignity of being called 'ecky becky' and 'red leg,' would speak to Charlie in the same patronising tone the white slave masters used in years past. However, he managed to compose himself, keeping in mind the purpose of his visit.

"Get to it, boy."

"Charles," Charlie interrupted. "It's like this Boss. Before my grandmother died, she told me that if our family was ever in any kind of trouble or needed any help, you were the person to come to. She said that you were the kindest person she had ever known and you had promised her that you would be there for us at any time. So here I am, Boss.

"You see, my aunt Amanda left a daughter with my grandmother and went off to the UK. Her daughter, my cousin Charlotte, is now sixteen years old and about to take her final school leaving exams. All these years, her school fees were being paid by someone unknown to us. But this has suddenly stopped and she's having to leave school and find a job. I was told by my mother that there might be a job here for Charlotte in your kitchen, but you see, Boss, this is out of the question. It's not what her mother or my grandmother would have wanted for her.

"Charlotte's a very bright girl and her ambition is to gain the best exam results to be able to enter university in the UK when she joins her mother or our very own university here on the island. My point, Boss is this: Since you're known to be so kind and all, would you be kind enough to help us continue with her school fees?"

"That's a tall order bo . . . , Charles. Do you know how much the school fees are?"

"Not really," said Charlie, "but I'm sure we can work something out. Maybe I could do some gardening for you on Saturdays and as Charlotte is so clever at schoolwork, maybe she could come to the house on Saturdays whilst I'm up here and give your grandchildren some lessons. Of course, she would have to bring my little sister Yvonne with her as she looks after Yvonne on Saturdays when Mama and Marcia go to the market."

On hearing her name mentioned and the prospect of going to the Big House to be with the two youngest Evans children, Yvonne shouted, "Yippee! I would get to play with Sam and Tilly!"

"Shut up" Marcia shouted, "how do you even know their names? None of this is about you."

Yvonne shouted back across the table, "Granny took me there sometimes, so there."

During the long explanation, neither Charlotte nor Aunt Maisie said a word. Deep inside, Charlotte was feeling hopeful. As she looked across the table at Charlie, she wondered how a boy of just nearly nineteen could be so full of wisdom, love, care for others, and a sense of responsibility. She had seen other boys in the neighbourhood Charlie's age running around like "bulls in China shops," bouncing from one girl to another, not doing any kind of work and even going down the criminal route. Not so with her cousin Charlie who had stuck to his apprenticeship and now had a steady job with a contractor.

Charlotte was filled with admiration and gratitude for Charlie. He was doing his best to save her from a life she did not want and from humiliation. He was also keeping his promise to their beloved grandmother. Charlotte thought of every prayer she could think of to make Charlie's plan work and vowed within her that no matter how things turned out, she would find a way of showing him her gratitude and to make him proud of her.

Charlotte waited expectantly for Aunt Maisie to respond to Charlie's plan. When at last Aunt Maisie spoke, after many huffs, sighs, and hummms, she asked what was Mr. Evans reply to all that Charlie had put to him.

Charlie said, "He more or less agreed but on the part about the lessons, he would have to speak to his family and in particular to the children's parents. They would need to see and speak with Charlotte."

Aunt Maisie said to Charlotte, "I hope you see all the trouble you're putting people through and are grateful?"

"I am Aunty, I am," Charlotte replied.

The week dragged by slowly with no further arguments between Aunt Maisie and Charlie or talks about Charlotte leaving school. The tension in the household seemed to be lessening, though there was still no confirmation from the Big House that Charlie's plan with Mr. Evans was settled, or when and if Charlotte would meet with the young Evans' couple to start giving school lessons to their children. But Charlotte remained hopeful.

On Friday as Charlotte got off the bus from school and headed towards home, she saw old Walley who was the handy man at the Big House, coming down the road. Walley had lived and worked at the Big House since he was a young man and before the white plantation owners sold up and left for England. He had occupied a small outhouse at the back of the Big House and he had continued with the Evans as he did prior to their ownership.

As Charlotte got closer to Walley, he told her he was just about to call at her aunt's house with a message from the Boss. The message was that everything was in place for the school fees and that Charlotte was to come up to the Big House to meet with the younger Mrs. Evans tomorrow morning. Charlotte thanked Walley and hurried home with the news and with a newness of spirit.

"Good evening, Aunt Maisie. I just saw Walley from the Big House and he gave me the message that Mr. Evans has agreed to pay my school fees and that I am to meet with young Mrs Evans tomorrow morning. He said he was on his way here to see you but since he saw me, he gave me the message instead. Is it still ok with you, Aunty?"

Aunt Maisie said. "You already know how I

feel about the whole situation, but let me tell you. Don't go up there and bring any shame on this family. And don't go agreeing to anything more than Charlie told them, lessons for the children and that's all. And you'll be bringing Yvonne along and not for any longer than an hour, you hear me?"

"Yes, Aunty," Charlotte replied.

She couldn't wait to tell Charlie the good news when he got home.

As the girls went to their beds for the night, they chatted for long hours before drifting off to sleep. Marcia updated Charlotte on the latest goings-on between her and Brian and how good it felt to walk holding hands with him and not be afraid of Mama finding out. Marcia had dreams of one day getting married to Brian, but not before she had become an established dress maker and dress designer.

Charlotte told Marcia how pleased she was for her and hoped that she too would one day be as happy as Marcia was. She said she felt that as her granny used to say, "The tide was turning in her favour." Thanks to Charlie she could continue to go to school and take her exams and hopefully, with good grades she could do her A levels which would enable her to go to university. Her dearest wish was that by then her mother would be in a position to send for her to join her in the UK. Charlotte knew that Marcia was no longer listening to her as she could hear the usual snoring sounds from Marcia beneath the sheets that covered her head.

Charlotte laid awake for much longer, wondering what approach she would take with the children when giving them lessons. She thought maybe she would use the same approach that was taken with her when she had extra lessons after school. Aunt Maisie had already wondered why the children would need extra lessons anyway since they were attending a posh private school. Charlotte had not concerned herself too much with that. She knew full well that Charlie had only made that offer to old Mr. Evans as a "carrot before the donkey" to soften him up.

Charlie had also told Mr. Evans that Granny had said he was a kind man who would do anything to help the family. This was also Charlie's tactic at softening up the old man and it seemed to have worked. Mr. Evans had agreed he would help with the school fees and there was no need for Charlie to do any work for the Evans. But Mr. Evans thought the lessons for the children were a very good idea.

CHAPTER 6

LESSONS AT THE BIG HOUSE

On Saturday morning, Charlotte woke up much earlier than usual. She knew that Aunt Maisie would also be heading to the kitchen to start a cooked breakfast for the family since Saturday and Sunday were the only two days they had time for such a breakfast. This usually consisted of fried plantains, eggs, and bakes (a batter of flour mixed with sugar, nutmeg, or spice and fried in oil). On occasions when flying fish were plentiful, there would be some left over from the night before. These would be served with the plantains, along with salt bread. As Charlotte entered the kitchen, she realised she was the only one up and decided that she would begin the breakfast.

The smell of frying brought Aunt Maisie rushing to the kitchen. To her surprise, Charlotte was standing at the stove. Aunt Maisie shouted to Marcia to come quickly. Marcia rushed to the kitchen her hand in one sleeve of her dressing gown and the rest of the gown hanging behind her.

"What's the matter, Mama?" Marcia said, thinking something had gone drastically wrong. Her mother exclaimed,

"Wonders never cease! Rain g'ine fall," an old phrase used when something out of the ordinary happened or was about to happen. "Charlotte making breakfast."

Charlotte smiled and continued the frying. Aunt Maisie joined her and began to mix the batter for the bakes.

"Couldn't you sleep or something?" she said to Charlotte.

"Not really, Aunty," Charlotte replied. "It's today I'm to meet with the Evans about giving lessons to their children and I'm a bit scared."

"What are you scared about? They're only small children. You just have to make them read and do a few sums. What's so difficult about that? Besides, you'll be taking 'know it all' Yvonne with you. I'm sure she will give them a run for their money."

"Do you think they would want me to start right away? I was thinking I would take along some of my old books I used to use when I was their age and a few crayons, just in case."

"Can't do any harm," Aunt Maisie said. "Just you be careful what you agree to and what you say. What happens in this house stays in this house."

After breakfast, Aunt Maisie and Marcia headed for the market in the city to collect the weekly supplies for the home. Charlotte got herself and Yvonne ready, with Yvonne asking a million and one questions about what they were going to do, and should she take along her latest doll Charlie had bought her. Charlotte told Yvonne they were not going to play but to learn.

"Ahh" Yvonne replied, "but I could keep it in my bag just in case."

"Okay," said Charlotte, "but you have to behave yourself and not touch anything in the house."

"I will and I won't touch anything, I promise" Yvonne said excitedly.

As Charlotte and Yvonne arrived at the Big House, they were met by Daisy the cook at the side door entrance of the house.

"Good morning," Charlotte said. "I'm here to see Mr. and Mrs. Evans."

"You must be Charlotte, since this little one is Yvonne." Yvonne was known by the cook and the Evans as she had made a few visits there with their grandmother. "Come in. You can wait in the dining room. The Boss is out but the master is in the study and Mrs. Evans is just getting ready. She should be down in a few minutes."

Charlotte entered the dining room, which seemed to her to be enormous and full of furniture she had only ever seen as she passed furniture shops in the city. Amongst the furniture was a long sideboard crowded with family photos. One of the photos caught her eye and it was as if the child in the photo was herself looking back at her. Charlotte shook her head hoping to dismiss the idea that the child in the photo could be her, but try as she might, she could not keep her eyes off that one photo.

The door to the dining room opened and Mrs. Evans appeared. She greeted Charlotte warmly and smiled at Yvonne, calling her 'Poppet' and asking her what mischief she had been getting up to.

"Nothing" Yvonne replied. "Where are Sam and Tilly? Can I show Tilly my new doll?"

Charlotte was mortified. She drew Yvonne closer to her and reminded Yvonne that they had not come to play. Mrs. Evans smiled.

"Don't worry, she's just being herself. Sam and Tilly will be down shortly. They're just getting dressed. And besides, not having them here gives us a chance to talk. Papa Evans said he thought you might be able to give the children some extra lessons and teach them how to keep focused in class. I think for their age they're doing okay, but they're easily distracted and often complain of being bored at school during lessons. Have you given any lessons before? Do you want to be a teacher when you finish school?"

Charlotte had not expected so many questions about herself in such a short space of time. She could only reply that she had not thought of what she wanted to do for a career, but was at the present time concentrating on getting through her exams with good grades. She said she had only had experience of teaching her cousin Yvonne and that when she was younger, she would help other children in class who were struggling.

Mrs. Evans said she must be doing a very good job with Yvonne as she seemed a very bright child with a very inquisitive mind. Charlotte replied that she was. From the corner of her eye she could see Yvonne anxiously moving from one leg to the other and looking in the direction of the stairs to see when Sam and Tilly would appear. Mrs. Evans said she knew Papa Evans had suggested that Charlotte come for an hour on Saturdays. She asked Charlotte if she was prepared to stay and have a trial run to see how the children would respond. Mrs. Evans had told the children that Charlotte was coming with Yvonne to give them lessons and that they needed to be well-behaved and attentive. The children had been more interested in Yvonne coming than in having lessons, Mrs. Evans informed Charlotte.

The children had met Yvonne on many occasions, unlike Charlotte who had never been anywhere near the Big House. She knew of her grandmother's visits there from time to time, but Charlotte had never met the young Evans or their children. She knew old man Evans because he had given her a lift to the city on her way to school a few times.

Charlotte agreed that she would spend some time with the children that morning as an introduction. She informed Mrs. Evans that by chance she had brought some of her primary school books she had used for her own after-school lessons. As Charlotte drew the books from her bag, Mrs. Evans smiled and said that the children had already passed that stage of reading. Nonetheless, it would be good for Charlotte to see how advanced they were and have an idea of what new things she could introduce to them.

As the maid brought the children into the dining room, they were introduced to Charlotte. Yvonne of course was ready to show off her new doll she had kept in her bag, but she caught the stern look from Charlotte and decided to keep quiet.

As the maid and Mrs. Evans left the room, Charlotte showed the children the books she had brought and asked them what they like best at school. Sam said he liked geography "because you learn about other countries of the world." Tilly said she liked reading, especially about children in other countries, but said she often got bored during other lessons. Yvonne said she liked doing sums. Sam said, "It's not called sums, it's math," and he hated it.

Charlotte decided that it might be a good idea to introduce the children to educational games and puzzles in all the different subjects, especially the subjects they found boring. That way there would be an element of play as well as improving on the subjects they didn't like and learning new ones.

As Mrs. Evans had suggested, Charlotte asked the children to read the books Charlotte had brought, as a guide to see what she would do with them in the future. Sam read first and, in a flash, had faultlessly completed the passage she gave him to read. Next, she gave Tilly a passage from another book that was a higher level than the one she gave Sam. To her amazement both children were heads above Yvonne in their reading skills.

Aunt Maisie was right, the children did not need to have extra lessons. Charlotte thought that the restlessness and boredom the children displayed at school must be due to them being further ahead of their peers at school and not being able to move at their own pace. She would have to be very careful in suggesting this to Mrs. Evans.

After all, the children were attending a posh private school, and what would Charlotte know?

For a number of weeks after that first introduction, Charlotte's lessons with the Evans' children and Yvonne continued. According to the children's mother, teachers at their school had reported a marked difference in the children's behaviour: the children had been more attentive in class and were no longer distracting others. Mrs. Evans also reported to Charlotte that the teachers thought it might have been due to the children being so far ahead of some of their peers in school and the pace of the lessons were too slow for them. They had asked the children's parents if they would agree to moving the children to a higher class along with a few of the other brighter children.

Charlotte had already come to this conclusion since her first meeting with the children, but had not had the courage to say so in case she might be thought to be too "uppish and full of herself." She was happy that the children's needs were now being properly met at school.

Aunt Maisie had also seen a change in Yvonne: she was now more eager to read books than play with dolls. She had actually spoken to her mother and brother about getting books for her Christmas presents rather than toys—although she said she would still like at least one toy or game.

CHAPTER 7

A LETTER FROM MOTHER

It was now almost two months since Charlotte had been visiting the Big House to give lessons to the children. The picture on the Evans' sideboard was still a puzzle to her. She had spoken to Marcia about it many times during their late-night chats. Marcia had always come to the conclusion that perhaps the picture looked a bit like Charlotte, and that Charlotte wanted it to be her so much that in her heart she believed it was.

It had been some time since Charlotte had written to or received a letter from her mother. She knew that Aunt Maisie had heard from her and had written back to inform her mother that Charlotte was being allowed to continue attending high school. Aunt Maisie had also informed her mother that Charlotte had taken her exams and was now giving lessons to the Evans' children at the Big House.

In Charlotte's last letter to her mother, she had asked if her mother was any nearer to seeing a way of bringing Charlotte to join her in the UK. Whether her mother had responded in her letter to Aunt Maisie, or in a letter to herself that had been intercepted by her aunt, Charlotte had no way of knowing. But either way, she had received no reply.

It often pained Charlotte that Marcia was allowed to have a boyfriend and some adult privileges. Even though they were of a similar age, Charlotte was not even allowed to see her mother's letters or write to her without her aunt's permission, or having her letters vetted by her aunt. Charlotte felt there was so much she wanted to say to her mother. She especially wanted to ask her about the picture of the girl on the sideboard at the Big House.

At last, the exam results were out: Charlotte had done exceedingly well. She was over the moon with her results, but it suddenly dawned on her that she had not thought beyond her CXC exams. *What now?* she thought to herself. She could go on to the sixth form at school to do her A levels or go to the community college to complete her education. Secretly, Charlotte had harboured the notion that by now her mother would have seen her way to have Charlotte join her in the UK.

One week after her exam results came out, Aunt Maisie summoned Charlotte to the front room for a private conversation. Charlotte wondered what she had done wrong since this was the usual procedure when Aunt Maisie wanted to chastise her for some wrong she thought she had done. On entering the room, she saw that Aunt Maisie was holding an open letter. Charlotte began to apologize, expecting her aunt to accuse her of writing to her mother again before running the letter passed her. She declared that she had not written to her mother.

Aunt Maisie told her to be quiet and listen. She had received a letter from Charlotte's mother earlier that day. Her mother had expressed her joy at Charlotte's exam results and with that she and her husband had begun to explore the possibility of bringing Charlotte to the UK to join them. They had made enquiries about Charlotte attending a sixth form college in England in September. *But that was less than two months away,* thought Charlotte. *Could preparations for her to travel to the UK and join a college be done in such a short time?*

Charlotte had stopped hearing all that her aunt was saying. She saw her lips moving but she was in a world of her own. The sound of her aunt shouting "Are you listening to me, girl?" brought her down to earth.

"Yes, Aunty, I hear you. Can all that needs to be done for me to go be done before September?"

"Have you never heard 'where there's a will there is a way'? It's been a long time in coming. You just need to get a passport."

At the mention of her getting a passport, Charlotte smiled, remembering the time Marcia's friend had told her she had an "Island passport."

"You'll also need a copy of your exam results to send to your mother. I can get Charlie to speak to old man Evans to speak to someone at the passport office to hurry it up, and you can get references from the Evans' children's parents and your school in case they're needed. Your mother and her husband can send you a letter of invitation. That's it. It shouldn't be too difficult."

Charlotte felt that Aunt Maisie was as eager to see her go as she was to be going. Aunt Maisie told her she would tell Charlie, Marcia, and Yvonne later that night. "You might need to let the parents of the children at the Big House know that plans are being put in place for you to travel before the end of September."

That night, Charlotte and Marcia chatted long into the night as they usually did before drifting off to sleep. That night seemed to take forever, although Marcia being always the chattier one was unusually quiet. Charlotte said to her, "Oh Marcia, can you believe it's really happening? I feel so blessed. First, I was allowed to finish school to take my exams. Then I got better results than I expected and now my mother has at last decided not only to have me join her in the UK but to enroll me at a college to do my A levels! Oh Marcia, things can't get much better than this. I wish Granny was still alive to see all she wished for me come to pass."

In the darkness of the room, Charlotte thought she could hear a sniffle coming from Marcia. Then she heard Marcia say, just above a whisper, "I'm going to miss you."

"I shall miss you too and dear Charlie, and Yvonne, the little minx," Charlotte replied.

Over the past couple of years the girls had grown very close and shared many things: Marcia sharing her dream of getting married to Brian and having her own dress-making and designing business; Charlotte wondering about the photograph she had seen in the Evans' house, her wish to join her mother and her sadness at the loss of their grandmother.

The girls rarely spoke of, or thought about, their fathers. Marcia, of course knew her father. He came and went in and out of the family home, as most of the men on the Island did. Her mother never complained when he came back to the family and would welcome him with open arms. A smack on her bottom was all Aunt Maisie needed to reassure her she was still her husband's number one woman. But during the time he was absent, when speaking of him to the children she would refer to him as "your no-good father."

Charlotte on the other hand had not known her father. Her mother had told Charlotte that her father had gone away, meaning overseas. She had always told Charlotte from the time she could understand that she didn't need a dad. She had her mother and Granny. So, like many of the children in the Island who never knew their fathers, she never thought or questioned who he might be, although since seeing the photograph on the Evans' sideboard, she had wondered if it had a link to who her father might be. Charlotte had once or twice entertained the notion that the younger Mr. Evans, Sam and Tilly's dad, might also be her dad, but his age didn't seem to fit. She had also toyed with the idea that it might even be old man Evans: was he the secret source paying her school fees up until her sixteenth birthday?

As the summer holidays were beginning at all the schools in the Island, Charlotte felt that now would be a good time to inform Mrs. Evans and the children that she was preparing to join her mother in the UK and that her last Saturday with the children would most probably be somewhere at the beginning or middle of August.

Mrs. Evans told Charlotte she was pleased for her and thanked her for the work she had done with the children. She knew that the children would miss Charlotte but most of all they would miss Yvonne coming with her on Saturdays. Mrs. Evans said she would tell her husband and Pa Evans, and of course prepare the children before her visit on Saturday.

With the help of Charlie and Marcia, Charlotte had completed the passport form. Aunt Maisie had instructed her to go to the picture studio in the city to have the 'ping pongs' (photographs) taken for her passport. Charlotte, Charlie, and Marcia had had a few laughs about how she looked in the passport photo. They thought it looked weird: no smile and staring. But it was good enough for the passport.

Later, when Charlie got home from work, he accompanied Charlotte to the Big House to have Mr. Evans witness and countersign the passport form. With that taken care of, all that was left to do was to send the copies of her exam results to her mother, and await the arrival of the passport and a letter of invitation from her mother stating that she was Charlotte's mother and would be her supporter. Plus, she needed the money for her plane ticket.

Everything seemed to be happening so fast. Charlotte was afraid to think about it being real in case it all slipped away. At night she prayed, "Dear Lord, let it be true and let nothing go wrong."

Sometimes, alone in her bedroom while Marcia was out with Brian, Charlotte would take her grandmother's Bible and search for passages to give her hope that nothing would go wrong and stop her going to join her mother. She remembered a passage in Hebrews that said, "Faith is the substance of things hoped for, the evidence of things not seen." Charlotte had heard sermons preached on it several times, but was unable to find which chapter it was.

Charlotte knew that faith meant believing for the things you wanted, but believing had so often been used in the wrong way by older people in the neighbourhood. She had once overheard Aunt Maisie gossiping with a neighbour as she sat at the window after dark, as Granny used to do. Aunt Maisie was telling how someone they knew had become a "believer," meaning she had become a born-again Christian.

Aunt Maisie had sarcastically quipped, "She believe? The only believe she believe in is obeyah," meaning the person they were gossiping about believed in witchcraft.

Charlotte smiled to herself but knew deep in her heart that her belief was her faith in God. He was showing Himself as the faithful father her grandmother told her He was. Granny had always reminded her that "those who God holds in His hands, none can snatch away." *She would stay strong,* Charlotte thought to herself, *and see all she was hoping for come to pass.*

The two weeks wait for the collection of the passport was finally up. It had been an anxious time for Charlotte, but at last the day had arrived for it to be collected. Things began to move swiftly again as on the same day the passport was to be collected, the postman knocked to say he had two letters and one was a signed-for letter for her aunt. Charlotte knew from the handwriting that the letter was from her mother which she hoped was the letter of invitation and the money for her passage. And sure enough, that's just what it was.

CHAPTER 8

THE FAREWELL PARTY

It was the middle Saturday in August and all the preparations for leaving the Island were almost complete. It was time to end the lessons with Sam and Tilly. As their mother had promised, she had prepared them for their last lessons with Charlotte. Today Charlotte would be saying goodbye to the children.

She knew that there would be lots of questions from Sam and Tilly, with her cousin Yvonne no doubt ready with all the answers. Charlotte also knew that today the children would not be very interested in lessons. So she had an idea: since the children were always interested in learning about foreign places and people, she would talk to them about what she knew of England and the British who had settled in the Island many years ago.

As she arrived, the children were already waiting for her. Before Charlotte could even begin the day's lesson, she was bombarded with lots of questions about her going to England. She was happy that she had brought along with her a book she had taken from the library with pictures of the first settlers on the Island. She told them that many years ago the British who came to the Island were the owners of the large plantations like the one they lived on, and that they called the Island "Little England" and called England "the Mother Country."

Sam said he already knew that because he had learned that at school. Tilly wanted to know why there were no white children in the plantation pictures, only black children and black workers. Yvonne said it was because they always stayed in the house because the sun was too hot and would turn then brown like she and Sam. Sam said that was stupid.

Sensing the restlessness in the children, Charlotte decided she would take them outside as it was not far off their play time. Just as they were about to head out the door, Mrs. Evans appeared followed closely behind by Daisy, the housekeeper, with glasses of lemonade. Mrs. Evans told Charlotte before she left that Pa Evans wanted to see her.

After the children had finished their drinks, Charlotte showed them a few more pictures of plantations around the Island that had been owned by white plantation owners who had returned to England. She continued to tell the children that England was a part of what is known as the United Kingdom because there were other countries attached to it, like the Island was part of the Caribbean, and also known as the West Indies.

After a while, Tilly said she wanted to know about children living in England and if she would be giving lessons to white children in England like she was doing with them. Charlotte explained that she was going to be with her mother and to finish her own education, so she could go on to university and become a professional person. She was not yet sure if she might become a doctor or nurse, but she was not going to be giving lessons to children.

It was almost time for the half-hour play-time she gave them outside before the lesson ended. She told the children that since this was her last lesson with them, they were allowed to have playtime a bit earlier. With this, the children headed outside, racing each other to the rope swing hanging from the golden apple tree at the back of the house. With the help of Walley, Pa Evans had made a rope and tyre swing for his grandchildren, just as he had done for his own children when they were younger.

While the children argued whose turn it was next for the swing and who should push, Charlotte took the opportunity to speak to Walley who was not very far away cleaning out the goat pens. She thought she would make one last ditch effort at getting some information from him about the photograph on the Evans' sideboard, and its links with Charlotte and her mother. But as usual, Walley avoided her line of questioning. He told her he was glad to hear that she would be joining her mother soon and she must remember him to her mother.

With that, Charlotte returned to the children. It was time for her to go. She hugged Sam and Tilly, wishing them goodbye. Making her way towards the dining room, she met Mrs. Evans who thanked her again for the time she had spent with the children. She reminded Charlotte that old Pa Evans wanted to see her before she left. Mrs. Evans said she would let him know that Charlotte was leaving.

As Pa Evans entered the room, Mrs. Evans said goodbye and left.

"I hear you have been doing a good job with the children," Pa Evans said.

Reaching into his pocket he pulled out an envelope. He handed it to Charlotte telling her it was a little something for the work and time she had spent with his grandchildren. Reluctantly, Charlotte took the envelope. Not knowing what to say, she stammered that she had not expected to be paid as her cousin Charlie had told her something had been worked out to allow Charlotte to continue school. She told Pa Evans that she was thankful for his help in making it possible. Shaking her hand, Mr. Evans wished Charlotte well and told her that her grandmother would have been very proud of her.

Charlotte called to Yvonne that they were leaving. Taking one last look around her in the yard of the Big House, Charlotte waved goodbye to Sam and Tilly.

On her return home Charlotte opened the envelope she had taken from Mr. Evans. The envelope contained $100, an amount of money she had never seen nor had ever been in the Beckles' household at any one time. Looking at the money,

Charlotte thought of all the things she could buy, but knew that it would be wrong to keep the money hidden from Aunt Maisie. With only three weeks before she was to leave the Island, the right thing to do was to hand the money over to Aunt Maisie.

As the family gathered at the table for the evening meal, Charlotte produced the envelope with the money given to her by Mr. Evans. She stated how much it was. Marcia and Charlie sat with open mouths and wide eyes declaring "How much?!" Aunt Maisie simply said, "Wonders never cease," and "guilty conscience don't let white ed-does stew." Charlotte pondered what the remarks meant but made no comment.

After the evening meal, Aunt Maisie began to prepare the mosquito spray of kerosene oil and DDT and the smouldering rags she placed in all corners of the house. This was her usual practice just before she settled down to sit at the window. She would watch as people passed by and engage in conversation with anyone who came to the window to listen to the latest radio saga of 'None so Blind' or to have a gossip with Aunt Maisie.

On such occasions, a row would often erupt between Aunt Maisie and Charlie as he got dressed and ready to meet his girlfriend for the cinema. Charlie would come out of his room smelling of Lifebuoy soap and 4711 Eu de Cologne. He could never understand why his mother went to such lengths to get rid of mosquitos and still sit with the window wide open letting them in! He complained that all she did was to stink up the house and that, far from killing the mosquitos, she was killing everyone in the house. He had even gone so far as tell his mother that one day she would burn the house down with the smut rag. With that he would walk through the door with his mother calling after him, "If you don't like it you know what you can do. You are not the man of this house!"

That night before going to bed, Aunt Maisie told the girls she had decided that she would use some of the money from Mr. Evans to give Charlotte a going away party, and spend some on the clothes she would need to travel in. At the mention of a party, Yvonne asked if she could bring her friends Sam and Tilly. Marcia shouted "Who asked you? Just be quiet."

Aunt Maisie told Yvonne that she could invite a couple of her friends, but it was Charlotte's party and Sam and Tilly definitely could not come.

"Why not?" asked Yvonne.

"Because I say so," came Aunt Maisie's curt reply.

With that, Yvonne ran off in tears.

Later as Yvonne came out to say goodnight, Charlotte explained to her that as it would be a night party, she didn't think Sam and Tilly would be allowed to come. That seemed to satisfy Yvonne and she took herself off to bed.

Aunt Maisie told the girls the kind of food she would need to prepare for the party. Since Aunt Maisie worked in a cook shop, preparing food for city workers, she knew where to buy the food at a cheaper price. Aunt Maisie said she would make up some macaroni pie, sweet bread, and some pound cake as well as sugar cakes for the children. She would get Charlie to get a few drinks and she would make a bucket of Kool Aid.

Aunt Maisie said everything was in place for Charlotte's travels, but she still needed to purchase the air ticket and get a leaving date. As Aunt Maisie and the girls headed for bed, she told them that tomorrow she would go to the airline office to sort out the flight. She would need to go to the post office to change the money Charlotte's mother had sent from England. Since she might be late back, they were to start the evening meal.

As usual Charlotte and Marcia chatted for a long period before finally falling to sleep. The topic of their conversation that night was all about Charlotte leaving within a matter of weeks. They said they could hardly believe the time had come. Charlotte said her one regret was that their grandmother was not there to see her go. They laughed when they remembered the first night they shared the room together after their grandmother's funeral, and how scared they both were. Charlotte said she had been especially scared having to sleep in grandmother's bed.

The night of the going away party finally arrived. Charlotte would be leaving for the United Kingdom the next evening. Aunt Maisie had prepared all the food. After her argument with Charlie about the kind of drinks to buy (her preference being all soft drinks, but Charlie had included beer), the family awaited the guests they had invited. There were a few of Marcia's friends, Charlie's girlfriend and her brother, Aunt Maisie's friends who gossiped outside the window, the pastor from the Mission Church, a couple of older women from the Mother's Union, and Charlotte's Sunday School teacher from the Methodist church where the girls attended on Sundays.

Charlotte had also invited two of the girls from her school. She did not really call them her best friends as she had always found it difficult to fit into any group because of her light skin tone and soft curly hair: the light skinned girls wanted her in their groups, while the darker-skinned children also expected her in their group. Failing to take sides, she would be shunned or called "poor great" or "eckey becky." The two girls she had chosen to invite also attended her Sunday School class at the Methodist church.

As the guests arrived, Charlotte greeted them and showed them to where Aunt Maisie was laying out the food on the table. Following the greeting, old Ma Gittens from the Mission Church handed Charlotte a parcel wrapped in white bread paper. She explained to Charlotte that the gift was a pair of cotton gloves she had kept in her trunk since she wore them to a wedding many years ago. Ma Gittens said she had washed and ironed them and since she knew that in England people wore gloves because of the cold, she thought it was a good gift for her. Charlotte thanked her and showed her to a chair in the front room.

As the evening wore on and all the invited people gathered, Aunt Maisie asked the pastor if he would say a prayer for Charlotte and bless the food. The pastor began by thanking God for the life of Charlotte and for blessing her with such a lovely family, especially her aunt who had always taken such good care of Charlotte since her mother left her and the death of her grandmother. He prayed that God would bless and keep the family she was leaving and the one she would be joining, that they would be as good to her as her aunt had

been. He also prayed that, although she had not
joined his congregation even though she had once
come forward after an altar call at the Mission
Church, he prayed that she would find her way to
the Lord and that she would make Him the Lord
of her life.

During the prayers, the old ladies from the
Mission Church and the pastor's wife said, "Amen"
and "Praise God." As the prayers came to a close,
Ma Gittens began to sing "God be with you till
we meet again." With this, Charlotte saw her aunt
standing across from her with tears rolling down
her cheeks. She was not sure what to think: were
they genuine tears and a feeling sadness at her
leaving, or brought on by the emotions exuded
by the song and the pastor's prayers? But never
before had she felt so moved and close to her aunt.
She instinctively wanted to throw herself into the
arms of her aunt as she did with her grandmother
when she was alive, but she controlled the urge
to do so as she knew Aunt Maisie was not a very
tactile person.

Often she had seen her shoo little Yvonne
away, telling her she had no time for "much ups."
The closest Yvonne would get to cuddles from
her mother was when she sat on the stool between her knees to have her hair braided and she
would fall asleep with her head on her mother's
knee. Aunt Maisie's excuse was always that she
was too busy. It pained Charlotte to see her aunt
standing there with tears in her eyes. It was then
Charlotte decided that regardless of whether or
not the tears were a feeling of sadness at her leaving, somehow she would find a way to let her
aunt know how grateful she was for the care she

had given her. Perhaps she would write her a letter before going to bed.

As the party went on, Aunt Maisie and the girls served the food of chicken, rice and peas, macaroni pie, sweet bread, and pound cake. Charlotte was given many unwrapped gifts mostly of toiletries made in England. Years later when she heard the phrase used "taking coals to Newcastle," she remembered this night: She would be taking things made in England with her to England.

Amongst the many gifts she given was a gold-coloured C-shaped broach, which Charlotte thanked the pastor's wife for, saying she would treasure it. She was also given a bright yellow sweater from the collection made on her behalf at the Methodist Sunday School and a bottle of Khus Khus perfume from Charlie's girlfriend. Old Walley from the Big House had also brought along a gift sent to her from Mrs. Evans, Sam and Tilly. It was a bottle of Avon "Here is My Heart" perfume. Charlotte was overjoyed by the many gifts she had received. She knew she would not be taking all of the toiletries with her and would decide in the morning what she would leave behind.

As the party came to an end, Aunt Maisie told Marcia and Charlotte to see Ma Gittens home a few houses away. Charlie had already left to take his girlfriend home, glad of the opportunity to get out into the fresh air of the night as the house had been so warm. The girls too jumped at the opportunity to leave the house.

On the way home, the girls chatted as they often did but this time was different. Charlotte said to Marcia, "Listen."

Marcia asked "To what?"

It was the night sounds of the crickets and whistling frogs which until now Charlotte had only ever found annoying. But tonight it was the sound of harmonious music to her ears. She wondered if she would hear such sounds in England. They both laughed as Marcia declared, "Only you would think of such a silly thing."

As they reached home, closing the wire wicket fence gate, Charlotte told Marcia to go on in without her as she wanted to stand outside for a little longer. As she did so, looking up at the sky that night it looked blacker than ever. With the darkness of the sky, each individual star seemed to shine brighter as if each one was trying to outshine the others.

Charlotte smiled to herself. She thought of her grandmother and wondered what she would be saying to her if she were there. Charlotte tried to shake any thought of sadness from her mind as she felt her grandmother would have been pleased that at last she was going to be reunited with her mother. Her thoughts were interrupted by the call from her aunt to come inside as it was time to help with the tidying up, and she needed to get to bed in preparation for the long flight ahead of her tomorrow.

Charlotte gathered together what she would take from the gifts she had been given: the C-shaped broach was definitely her favourite - as that letter started her name - as were the cotton gloves from Ma Gittens. The rest of the gifts she would give to Marcia and Aunt Maisie. She knew that her aunt would be careful not to let Yvonne know that Charlotte had given her some of the gifts as it was quite possible that Yvonne would spread it around, and it would be hurtful to those who, out of the kindness of their hearts, had taken the trouble to gift them to Charlotte.

Having only recently had electricity installed in the house, Charlotte knew that Aunt Maisie would probably not want her to stay up to write letters as she was very cautious of how the electricity was used and of the electricity bill. She would wait until she thought everyone was asleep and write the letters from her bed by the electric light that hung from the bedroom ceiling. She knew that once Marcia had gone to sleep hardly anything woke her up.

In her letter to Aunt Maisie, Charlotte poured out her gratitude to her aunt for all that she had done for her, especially since the death of her grandmother. She was grateful also to Charlie for his help in negotiating with Mr. Evans for the payment of her school fees to allow her to continue school to the end of her exams. She expressed her love for her cousins, Marcia and Yvonne, and how much she was going to miss them, but said that she would write often. With that, Charlotte closed the letter which she would slip under the door of Aunt Maisie's bedroom before they left for the airport.

CHAPTER 9

THE UK

Having had a very restless night, Charlotte got up early in the morning in time to see Charlie before he left for work. As he was leaving, Charlotte hugged him closely with tears in her eyes. Charlie told her, "None of that. Be happy you are leaving this place."

Charlie promised Charlotte that he would drop by the airport if he finished work in time to see her before she boarded for her flight. He said that he had arranged with Walley to take Charlotte, his mother Marcia, Yvonne, and his girlfriend Lorna to the airport. The Big House van was big enough to take them and her luggage. With that, he left her standing at the door.

At that point, everyone was awake and the house seemed busier than ever. Aunt Maisie made breakfast. She said there was no need to cook lunch before they left for the airport as there was enough left over rice and chicken from the party. Aunt Maisie wanted them to be leaving the house by 11:30 or noon at the latest. She fretted that Charlie had made arrangements with Walley to use the Evans' 'jalopy' as she had seen it on the road going at snail's pace. Aunt Maisie would have been quite happy to pay a taxi to take them to the airport. Aunt Maisie told Marcia she was to go to the Big House at 10:30 to remind Walley he was to be at the house at 11:30 sharp.

Throughout the morning, Aunt Maisie kept reminding Charlotte to make sure she had the passport in her handbag, constantly asking Charlotte if her case was all packed and labelled and if she left the sweater out to wear on the plane (as Aunt Maisie had heard that it got very cold on airplanes).

When Walley arrived sharply at eleven o'clock, Aunt Maisie and the girls were just finishing off clearing away the lunch dishes. Aunt Maisie asked Walley if he wanted to eat while warning him that he would have to eat it quickly. Walley said he would and did so as the girls and Aunt Maisie got dressed.

By 11.45, they were all loaded into the van and on the way to the airport. As the van rolled along the road to Seawell airport, no one spoke except Aunt Maisie to ask one more time if Charlotte had her passport.

As they drove along, Charlotte kept her eyes on the palm trees by the roadside swaying in the breeze like marching sentinels. With mixed feelings of excitement and sadness, she threw her arms around Yvonne who was sitting between her and Marcia. As she did so, Yvonne began whimpering, which quickly turned into loud sobs until Aunt Maisie shouted at her to stop her foolishness.

Having reached the airport in plenty of time, Charlotte looked around to see if Charlie had arrived to see her off as he had promised, but he was nowhere to be seen. Her heart sank as she was counting on him for the strength and courage she needed to say her last goodbyes to her family. Charlotte knew that with Charlie there she would hold it together. As she continued to look around, Aunt Maisie hurried her along to the check-in desk with Walley following behind with the luggage.

Minutes before she was due to go through the departure gate, Charlotte caught sight of Charlie hurrying towards them. As he approached, Charlotte threw her arms around him burying her head in his chest and began to cry uncontrollably. Releasing her arms from around his neck, he apologised for his late arrival and told Charlotte not to be sad as going to join her mother was the best thing that could happen for her. Aunt Maisie agreed with him and told her it was time for her to be going.

As Charlotte reached out to hug Aunt Maisie goodbye she saw tears rolling down Aunt Maisie's cheeks. Charlotte clung to her aunt with a lingering hug until, releasing herself from Charlotte, Aunt Maisie turned away wiping her eyes. Charlotte reached out to Marcia with one hand around her neck and the other drawing Yvonne to them. The three girls hugged, sobbing for a while as they expressed their sadness at her leaving and how much they were going to miss each other. Charlotte walked towards the departure gate waving as she went until she could no longer see her family.

As Charlotte boarded the plane, she was shown to a window seat. Shortly after she was seated, a little girl no more than about six years of age was brought to sit next to her. The flight attendant smiled at Charlotte as she buckled the child into her seat. As she did so the stewardess whispered to the little girl that the nice young lady next to her would take good care of her. Charlotte smiled as she buckled herself into her own seat.

As the flight attendant left, Charlotte tried to engage the child in conversation, but the child only responded by shaking her head. Charlotte told the little girl that it was also Charlotte's first time on an aeroplane and that she was excited to be going to see her mother. She could see the child had been crying and was still looking very scared. Charlotte thought she would leave any further interaction with the child until after take-off.

Charlotte settled herself and gazed through the window. Moments earlier she had been glad of the momentary distraction of talking to the child seated next to her. It had taken her thoughts away from her own sadness at leaving her family behind. As she gazed through the window of the plane she could see the palm trees blowing in the wind just as they had been doing when she drove to the airport.

As she sat waiting for the plane to take off, Charlotte thought of her grandmother and wondered what she would have said now that the day had come for her to join her mother. She knew that although her grandmother would have been happy that she was going, she would no doubt have been sad to see Charlotte go. Charlotte knew in her heart that leaving her grandmother would have been for her the most difficult thing she ever had to do.

As the plane taxied along the runway preparing to lift off, Charlotte saw the child next to her stiffen as she gripped the armrest between them. She patted the child's arm whispering, "Don't be afraid. It's okay. We're about to take off and soon we'll be on our way to England." She realised the words she was speaking were as much to calm her own fears as they were the child's.

Charlotte turned her thoughts back to the family she had just hugged goodbye. She even thought of Sam, Tilly, and Yvonne, comparing them to the child sitting next to her. She thought of the forward and outspoken nature of the three children she had spent so much time with and how eager and fascinated they were to learn and explore new things. Would they have been as scared and silent as the child sitting beside her?

Soon they were in flight and on their way. As the plane levelled off, the attendant came to the child bringing her a colouring book and crayons. She smiled at Charlotte as she turned away. The captain spoke on the intercom welcoming them on board and informing them of the number of passengers and crew and time of expected arrival. Minutes later people on board began to move around the plane. The flight attendant came again to the child, asking if she was okay and if the nice lady was looking after her. The child nodded.

This time the flight attendant did not just smile at Charlotte but actually spoke to her, telling Charlotte that the little girl was on her way to join her parents in Birmingham. Charlotte smiled saying she too was on her way to join her mother in London. "How nice," the attendant remarked.

Handing Charlotte two menus the stewardess asked if she would be so kind as to fill one out for the little girl. The child had remained silent as Charlotte tried to engage her in finding out what she would like to eat from the menu. All she got were head motions so she decided to take a chance at ordering for the child what she ordered for herself.

As she did so there was a sudden jolt of the plane and the captain's voice announced that there was some turbulence and everyone was to stay seated and buckled up. The child began to whimper and with every jolt of the plane she screamed, "It's going down, it's going down!" Charlotte reached across the seat hugging the child as closely as she could, telling her it was okay and it would soon stop.

Charlotte could feel herself shaking with fear. She suddenly remembered the scripture her grandmother had always quoted: "Those whom God holds in His hands none can snatch." While she held the child, she thought of every scripture she had ever read, including Psalm 91. That is the passage of scripture the pastor had read at her leaving party stressing "He shall cover thee with His feathers and under His wings you shall take refuge." Thinking on this, she could feel herself and the child relaxing.

Not realising the turbulence had subsided for some minutes, she had kept hold of the child when she felt a tap on her shoulder asking her what they had chosen for the meal. Charlotte watched the child eat her food with relish while Charlotte barely ate her own—still feeling queasy from the turbulence moments ago. At the end of the meal and for the first time, the child spoke to indicate she needed to go to the toilet. Both Charlotte and the child joined the queue for the lavatory.

On their return, her young charge seemed more relaxed and ready to talk. She told Charlotte her name was Lucy and that she was called Lucy because she was born in the parish of St. Lucy. Charlotte laughed and remembered Sam, Tilly, and Yvonne as it was just the kind of forthright information they would have volunteered. Charlotte felt ashamed for earlier having negatively compared Lucy to Sam, Tilly, and Yvonne.

Settling themselves again, buckled and blanketed Lucy began to use her colouring book. Charlotte reclined her seat and closing her eyes, she began to visualise her meeting with her mother, half-brothers, and stepfather. In a matter of hours she would be with them. Would her longing and eagerness to be reunited with her mother and new family be all she was hoping it to be? Charlotte felt a restlessness in her spirit and again sought words of scripture and the words of encouragement she had always been given by her grandmother to calm her.

Turning towards Lucy, she noticed that she had fallen asleep. Putting away the colouring book and folding away Lucy's table, Charlotte reclined Lucy's seat and gently placed the blanket up around her shoulders, leaning the child's head against her own shoulder.

They both slept until the cabin lights came on and she felt a tap and a voice saying 'Breakfast.' "Gosh," she mumbled "that time already?"

Charlotte remembered hearing someone say before she left the Island that when the lights come on, it means an hour before landing. Rousing herself and gently coaxing the child awake, her stomach began to summersault with fear and anticipation. She tried her best to stave off all the negative thoughts that arose in her mind. *What if it didn't work out, what if her stepfather and brothers didn't like her, what if her mother had changed what if, what if?*

Charlotte's thoughts were soon interrupted as Lucy asked if she would take her to the toilet. Thankful for the intrusion into her thoughts, Charlotte unbuckled herself and Lucy and headed for the lavatory. It took a while to gain access to the toilets as passengers were queuing up to make ready for landing.

During their wait in the queue, Charlotte began a conversation with a fellow passenger, a young woman who told her she was a frequent visitor to the Island to see her grandparents. Both the young woman's own parents had left the Island years ago and she had been born in the UK. She loved the Island and never understood why her parents had chosen to leave and reside in the UK. They both smiled.

The young woman wanted to know if Charlotte was the little girl's mother. Charlotte said," Gosh no. I only met her on the plane. She is travelling alone to join her parents in Birmingham. I think the flight attendant was meant to be looking after her but I got given that task for some reason. But she is a sweet little thing."

"Here we go, my turn," the young woman said, and with that their conversation ended.

Settling back into their seats, passengers

were instructed to put away their blankets and headphones and stay seated with seat belts fastened for landing. Within seconds Lucy began to scream again. This time it was from the discomfort in her ears, which had affected many of the children on board. The attendant returned to the child with sweets and handing Charlotte a disposable cup with a warm paper towel, she asked if Charlotte would mind holding it against Lucy's ears if she would let her. This seemed to do the trick of reducing the pain and discomfort Lucy was experiencing.

At last with a thud, the plane landed. Even though instructed to remain in their seats until the seat belts signs were off, many passengers ignored this and began to remove overhead luggage and to stand in the aisle. At this point, the flight attendant who was meant to be looking after Lucy came and removed her from her seat taking her to the front of the plane—not smiling or thanking Charlotte for the attention she had given to Lucy.

Unphased by this, Charlotte concentrated on the instructions her mother had given her about what to do when she disembarked. She was to follow the other passengers who headed for the immigration queue and have her documents and passport ready, and also to look for the flight number to see which conveyor belt her luggage would be coming to.

On leaving the airplane, Charlotte felt the sudden change in the temperature. She shuddered and pulled her cardigan tightly to her body. She thought, *If it feels so cold and I'm still under cover, what must it be like on the outside? And it's still only September!*

Clutching her passport and the documents her mother told her she might need to hand over, Charlotte followed passengers as they made their way to the immigration desk. She also knew what she was to say her purpose for coming to the UK was. Thankfully, she cleared Immigration with no awkward questions or holdups and headed for the luggage collection point. She breathed a sigh of relief and thanked God for her safe journey so far.

As Charlotte stood waiting to collect her luggage, she once again resumed a conversation with the young woman she had met in the queue for the lavatory on the plane. The young woman told her she was heading for her parents in Berkshire and then on to her university campus in Reading. Wishing Charlotte good luck, she collected her luggage and waved her goodbye.

Charlotte struggled to remove her case from the carousel and fortunately a man standing nearby assisted her. Thanking him, she lifted the case on to a luggage trolley and began to make her way to the exit. Ahead of her were two signs marked 'to declare' and 'nothing to declare' and for a moment she wondered which one she should take. Remembering that her aunt had packed flying fish and a bottle of rum in her case for her mother, with her heart thumping she walked through the 'nothing to declare' exit and passed the customs officer.

She had passed almost every hurdle she was expecting to encounter with one last one to go, which was recognising the family waiting for her at arrivals. Although her mother had sent a recent photo of herself with her husband and her half-brothers and she had them imprinted in her memory, Charlotte remained nervous.

Walking through the arrivals hall to the waiting barrier, she saw her name held up on a signboard and shouts of "Charlotte!" coming from where the sign was. Within seconds she was in her mother's arms as tears began to flow from both of them. Memories came flooding back of the time she had stood at the wharf-side hugging her mother goodbye as she was about to board the boat taking her from the Island more than ten years ago.

After what seemed like forever hugging her mother, she was eventually introduced to her step-father and to her half-brothers. The boys, now six and four, hid behind their father's legs, not wanting to say hello to Charlotte. They were both anxious to get moving, asking if they could get their hot chocolate and doughnuts now. Prompted by their mother to greet their sister, the boys continued to hang behind their father's legs, still insisting that they wanted to go for hot chocolate.

Charlotte's mother handed her a warm coat telling her she looked frozen. They entered the coffee shop and the boys quickly clambered on to the seat, giving their father their orders for hot chocolate and doughnuts. Charlotte was asked what she would like but she declined and said she had had breakfast on the plane. Her mother prompted her to have a hot drink as the drive home would be up to an hour depending on the traffic. Charlotte accepted.

As she watched her brothers tuck into their food and drink, she wondered at their behaviour. She realised they were still very young but she could not help thinking they seemed impudent, demanding, and somewhat spoilt. She scolded herself for making such an assessment so soon, telling herself she would need to get to know her brothers and how they were disciplined by their parents.

They left the coffee shop and headed for home. Charlotte sat between the two boys and tried to interact with them but they continued to ignore her, at times reaching across her to snatch and grab toys from each other. Her mother constantly had to shout at them to behave and be nice for their sister.

Along the route, Charlotte was amazed to see the houses all joined together, unlike the houses on the Island which were separated by their own guard walls and fences. She was even more amazed to see smoke bellowing from the roof tops of the houses. She plucked up the courage to ask what the smoke from the house tops meant. Leaning between the front seats of the car towards Charlotte in the back, her mother explained that the smoke was coming from chimneys of houses that burnt coal in fire hearths to keep the houses warm and heat water.

Charlotte exclaimed in surprise, "You mean they actually burn fires inside houses?" Her mother explained that in some houses there were fireplaces in every room, but most modern houses were now built without fireplaces and chimneys because they used gas central heating. Some older houses like theirs were converted to central heating which was much cleaner and easier to manage and was able to heat all the rooms in the house at once as well as the water. Charlotte felt relieved—she could not imagine not having hot water on hand in such a cold place.

They reached the house and the boys could not wait to get out of the car, running ahead of their parents before they could even open the door. Charlotte was astonished at the appearance of the houses on the tree-lined street: all the houses appeared to be joined together and looking alike. She wondered how anyone knew which was their own house, except that they were numbered and a few front gardens were different.

When they entered the house Charlotte was embraced by the warmth that enfolded her and the cosiness of the house. Her mother helped her out of her coat whilst reminding the boys not to throw their coats on the floor.

Soon Charlotte was given a tour of the house and shown to her own room. The room was beautifully decorated with pink floral wallpaper. There was a single bed with the prettiest cover she had ever seen. Next to the bed was a small vanity chest and there was also a little desk with a reading lamp, a clock, and a small, framed photo of Charlotte sitting on her grandmother's knee.

Charlotte smiled as she looked at that picture. It brought back memories of the day her grandmother had taken her into the city to have the picture taken, telling her to smile nicely as she was sending it to her mother in England. How long ago that seemed now.

On the floor beside the desk was a wash basket and over the bed hung two pictures: one a photo of Charlotte as a young child and the other was a picture of Jesus at the Last Supper. Gazing at the picture of herself over the bed, Charlotte recalled her curiosity and confusion at seeing the exact same photo on the Evans' sideboard at the

Big House. She now knew that someday soon she would get the chance to ask her mother why the Evans had a picture of her.

As she was leaving Charlotte to get used to her room, her mother told her she could either have a shower before coming down to join them for what she called 'brunch' (as it was way past breakfast time and much nearer to lunch) or she could have a rest, "but not for too long." Her mother advised Charlotte that because of the jet lag, she should stay awake for as long as she could so she would be able to sleep when she went to bed for the night.

As her mother turned to leave the room, one of the boys came running in, complaining that he had been punched by his brother. Charlotte saw her mother smile and cuddle her brother while making no attempt to establish what had happened to make one of the boys punch the other. Once again Charlotte had her misgivings about the behaviour of the boys and of the kind of discipline they were given—so different from the way children were raised on the Island. But again, she told herself it was far too soon to make those judgments.

Her mother left the room and Charlotte decided that she would join the family for the breakfast/lunch. Her stepfather, James, was in the kitchen preparing the meal. Charlotte joined them at the table. James brought to the table individual plates of food announcing to Charlotte that this was her first English breakfast of sausages, eggs, beans, and mushrooms. Charlotte thought of the normal breakfast she would have had at Aunt Maisie of eggs and bread, or bakes and plantain, in contrast to what was being placed before her. Soon they all joined hands as James blessed the food and thanked God for bringing Charlotte safely to them.

While they ate, her stepfather suggested to Charlotte that she could choose what she wanted to call him. He said her mother called him 'Dad' like the boys, and he called her mother 'Mum.' He said he didn't mind if she called him 'Uncle' until she got to know him better and felt comfortable enough to call him Dad, but as from today she would be his daughter.

Charlotte smiled and expressed her thanks. She had not given any thought to this issue before joining them and she felt a little uneasy as it had taken her by surprise. She pondered briefly what she would do, eventually deciding that for the time, Uncle would feel more comfortable and appropriate.

Before taking her shower and going for a short rest, Charlotte asked if she could use the phone to call Aunt Maisie's neighbour to let her aunt and the others know she had arrived safely. She remembered that she had promised her aunt that she would let them know as soon as she arrived. With the help of her mother, she managed the long-distance call to her aunt's neighbour who was excited to be receiving a call from overseas and wanted to know if she should call Aunt Maisie to the phone. Charlotte declined the offer but told her to let her aunt know that she had arrived safely and would be writing to her as soon as she had settled.

The rest of the day passed quickly with the boys constantly squabbling and seeking their mother's attention. Evening drew to a close and although it was 6 p.m., Charlotte was surprised to see that it was still much lighter outside than it would have been at home on the Island at that hour. Her mother explained that the clocks would soon change for the winter and that mornings would then be lighter and the evenings darker.

After dinner, Charlotte, her mother, and James settled down to watch TV before going off to bed, the boys having gone up at 7.30 p.m. Before long, Charlotte felt she could no longer keep her eyes open and asked if it was okay for her to go to bed. Her mother replied that of course it was okay, apologising for not suggesting it earlier as Charlotte must be 'very jet lagged.' She reminded Charlotte that they were going shopping in the morning as she needed to get outfitted for the winter and for college.

CHAPTER 10

THE CHURCH VISIT

Within seconds of going to bed, Charlotte could feel herself drifting off to sleep. She struggled to stay awake long enough to say her prayers and thank God for bringing her safely to join her mother. She briefly thought of Marcia and how she would be feeling in their bedroom without her.

When she next opened her eyes, the clock beside her bed was saying 6:30 a.m. The house was very quiet but there was a strange sound coming from the street outside her window, a strange humming and clinking. Wondering what it could be, she moved to the window and took a look. It was a strange small vehicle loaded with milk crates. As it drove off, it made the humming noise—a pleasant noise, she thought. Returning to her bed, she began to think of the family she had left on the Island and a feeling of homesickness rose in her stomach.

Charlotte was roused by a knock on her door. "Rise and shine," a voice called. Popping her head into the room, Charlotte's mother, Amanda, asked if she had had a good night and was she ready to come down for some breakfast. Glancing at the clock beside her bed Charlotte realised that she had fallen asleep again for two hours since hearing the sound of the milk wagon. She apologised to her mother for sleeping so late but Amanda replied, "No need to apologise. We always have a bit of a lie in at weekends, although the boys always make sure it's not for too long! Take your time. Dad is making breakfast."

Showering and dressing hurriedly, Charlotte came down the stairs. Her brothers were already sitting at the table in the dining room and her mother and stepfather were in the kitchen. She said good morning to the boys, tussling the older brother's hair as she moved towards the kitchen to greet her stepfather. The boys just stared at her in silence.

"Good morning, Uncle. Sorry I overslept."

"You didn't," came the reply, "You did well to be up at this time. Eight hours flying is no joke. Sit yourself down, breakfast won't be a minute."

With that Charlotte returned to her brothers at the table. Try as she might to engage them, the boys remained silent and continued to play with their knives and forks. As her mother came to the table with the breakfast for the boys, she asked them if they had said good morning to their sister. It felt good for Charlotte to hear her mother refer to her to the boys as their sister. It made her feel included and gave her a sense of belonging, of being a part of the family.

With breakfast in front of everyone, they held hands and grace was said just as it had been at the meal times the day before. During the meal, Charlotte asked if she could have some writing paper as she had promised to write to Aunt Maisie as soon as she arrived. Apart from letting her know that she had arrived safely, Charlotte felt like she had so much to tell them, although she had only been in England for a few hours.

Before breakfast was finished, Charlotte mentioned that she had heard a strange humming and clinking of bottles on the street outside her window about six in the morning and wondering what it could be she had looked out the window. She'd seen a man carrying milk up the driveway and a vehicle loaded with crates of milk. She must have fallen asleep after she got back to bed.

James explained that it was the milk float which delivers milk every morning and soon she would also hear the rag-and-bone man and the coal truck as it delivered coal to the houses that were still using coal. Charlotte asked what was 'rag and bone.' She was fascinated by what she was being told. Her mother interrupted telling them they needed to finish up as they would need to get ready soon to go shopping to outfit Charlotte with some warm clothes and to get her some college supplies. She only had less than three weeks before starting college.

Her mother told Charlotte that Saturday was usually taken up with food shopping and making preparation for Church on Sundays. She was told that the family spent most of Sunday at church.

Her stepfather told her that after the morning service everyone stayed at church for lunch which was provided by the congregation. It was a chance to fellowship and get to know each other and find out how everyone's week had gone.

Charlotte commented that it must be a very small church to be able to cater lunch for the whole congregation. "Far from it," James replied, "the church is pretty large, but everyone chips in with the food and brings a different dish. It's quite fun and exciting especially for the children. It's as much a surprise for the children as the adults seeing what the different dishes are going to be laid on. It is especially so at Christmas time, so you have come at the right time."

Her mother said "You will get a chance to meet lots of people tomorrow and as we'll be looking to make preparations for the Christmas activities, you might be asked to help. Would you like that?"

On Sunday morning Charlotte woke up with a feeling of excitement and apprehension. After the business of the morning and everyone getting ready for church, they finally left the house. With the car loaded with the family and the food her mother and stepfather had prepared, they set off.

The boys chatted ninety to the dozen about what they were going to do with their friends, whilst Charlotte sat quietly wondering what the day held for her. She knew that her mother and stepfather had some part to play in the church ministry, but as yet she did not know the extent of their involvement.

As they left the car and prepared to enter

the church, Amanda hugged Charlotte and told her she looked worried. "But don't worry" she said comfortingly, "I'm sure you will be warmly welcomed. I have already mentioned to the congregation that my daughter was coming from the West Indies to join us." That made Charlotte feel even more nervous as she felt many eyes would be on her.

The church was a large building not typical of any of the church buildings she had ever attended: no stained-glass windows or tall steeple. It looked more like the Big House the Evans lived in back on the Island, but with rows of red velvet seats and altar upholstery.

Bracing herself for what was to come, Charlotte gingerly followed her family into the church. There were lots of handshakes and hugs and introductions to a number of the congregation. Sitting between her mother and her stepfather, Charlotte settled herself and waited for the service to begin.

Midway through the service an announcement was made for the welcoming of newcomers and Charlotte was asked by her mother and stepfather to stand up and say who she was. Timidly, she rose to her feet, and as she did so there was lots of hand clapping and shouts of "Welcome Charlotte," and "God bless you."

Settling again to her seat the service continued. Her mother read the lesson and to Charlotte's surprise, her stepfather conducted the sermon. At the close of the sermon, the announcements were made for the upcoming activities and an invitation for helpers to get things ready for the Christmas activities. Then an announcement was made for the usual Sunday preparation for the lunch and supervision of the children. With this the service came to a close. Charlotte was somewhat relieved as it seemed to go on forever.

Having still been a little nervous about what to expect at lunch, Charlotte was relieved to find that the lunch was an amazing experience. After a long prayer for grace and another welcome mention of Charlotte, everyone began to choose their selection of food from the many different dishes on display. Some of the food she had never heard of or seen before. Everyone appeared happy and friendly.

As the lunch ended, her mother and stepfather mingled a little and introduced Charlotte to a few more people. In the course of the many introductions, Charlotte was invited to take part in the children's ministry and to help with the activities that were being prepared for the Christmas programme. Charlotte nodded and smiled, indicating it would give her pleasure to do so.

When they returned home, Charlotte was asked how she thought the day had gone and if she had enjoyed herself. She replied that it was better than she had expected as she was a bit nervous to begin with. Charlotte commented on how well she thought her brothers had behaved. James said to the boys, "You hear that guys? Your sister thought you were very good today."

After helping her mother to pack away and clean up the dishes they had taken to church, Charlotte excused herself and went to her room. Throwing her shoes off and lying across the bed, she began to reflect on the day and on the many things she would have to write in her letter to Marcia.

Exhausted from the day, within minutes she fell asleep until she heard a knock at the door. Not realising she had been asleep so long, she rose from her bed only to find the older of her brothers standing at the door. He told her that Mum had asked if she was coming down for a snack. Charlotte bent to the level of her brother and patting him on his head said "Yes. That's so sweet of you to let me know. Tell Mum I'll be right down." She was surprised that her brother had taken his first step in connecting with her by bringing her the message from their mum, and that at last there was beginning to be a connection in her relationship with her brothers. "Small steps" as her grandmother would say.

Charlotte joined the others who were having a snack at the dining table. She apologised for not coming down earlier but explained that she had only meant to have a lie down but had fallen asleep. Again, she was told not to apologise as it was expected that she would still be jet lagged and that it had been a long day at church.

Before taking the boys off to bed, Charlotte was reminded by her mother that tomorrow would be another busy day for her. She was to attend a brief interview at the college since her course was due to commence in two weeks. *Another heart thumping day,* Charlotte thought, but one she felt sure would move her on to her future and one she had thought about for so many years: the completion of her education in Great Britain.

As Amanda left to attend to the boys for bed, Charlotte chatted with her stepfather who told her about his role at the church and at the college. He was a tutor at the college and it was there he had met her mother when she began her further education before becoming a nurse. It was his influence with the college and her excellent CXE grades that had enabled Charlotte to secure a place at the opening of term in September.

Charlotte thanked James for his help in making it possible. It reminded her of Charlie and all he had done to enable her to complete her CXEs when Aunt Maisie had contemplated sending Charlotte to work as a maid at the Big House. She thought of the many chances she had been given in her yet young life. She held on to the belief that there were yet many more to come.

Before settling for the night, Charlotte thought now would be a good time to write a letter to Aunt Maisie and Marcia. Taking the blue airmail letter forms her mother had given her from the desk by her bed, she proceeded to write.

Dear Aunt Maisie,

Greetings to you and all at home. I trust you and the others are all well and missing me as much as I miss you. Hopefully you got the message I sent you when I called to let you know that I had arrived safely.

As I write to you now, it is my third day since my arrival and I guess by the time this letter reaches you a week would have passed.

So far things have gone well. Mum and Uncle send greetings and thanks for the fish and the rum you sent them, although I am not so sure about the rum as I think my uncle might be a pastor or something. They seem very religious. We spent almost the whole of day at church yesterday. The church is busy preparing for their Christmas activities, and I have been asked if I would like to join the Children's Ministry. You know I am always up for anything involving children so needless to say I said yes.

Tomorrow, I have an interview at the college I am to attend. So, I will be getting myself ready for bed now but will write again soon.

I have so much to say about the flight and about meeting with Mum and my new family, but as you already know the space on these letter forms is at a premium and can only hold so much.

Thank you, Aunty, for everything. I will write again soon. Take care of yourself and give my love to everyone,

Much love,
Charlotte

Closing the letter, she rested her chin on the desk, her thoughts were on the family she had left behind on the Island. She especially thought of Marcia and wondered how she was coping without her. Charlotte thought of their many long chats at bedtime and she knew that she would miss them perhaps more than Marcia, who would often drift off to sleep during their conversation. Charlotte wondered about Marcia now having to share the room with Yvonne, which Aunt Maisie had already planned before Charlotte left.

She heard a knock on the door as her mother called "Goodnight Charlotte." Opening the door Charlotte reached towards her mother hugging her goodnight.

"Thank you for today, Mum."

Embracing her daughter tightly, Amanda felt the years of emptiness and longing to hold her daughter drain away. She replied, "Glad you enjoyed it. Sleep well, my precious."

Suddenly Charlotte remembered hearing that before: as a young child her mother would call her Precious and would often do so when lying next to her as they went to bed at night.

CHAPTER 11

DAD

Within a few short months, Charlotte had formed a bond with her mother, stepfather and her young brothers. Things were so different now between her and the boys. Often they would seek her out to read them stories and to hear her tell them about the children and places on the Island.

They particularly liked to her tell them how scared children on the Island were when it rained with thunder and lightning. People used to say that meant the devil and his wife were fighting. The older of the two boys would say, "That's stupid, the devil doesn't have a wife" and the two boys would argue until Charlotte said no more stories if they were going to keep fighting.

At this the boys would stop and ask her for one more story about how the doves cooing at midday sounded like the tune of the song 'Moses speak God's word.' With this they would roll over in fits of laughter when their sister cooed like the doves.

Amanda could not believe the change in her sons and the beautiful relationship that was growing between them and their sister. When she first saw them curled up next their sister on her bed as Charlotte read to them, Amanda was surprised. She was also surprised at how quickly Charlotte had settled into the family and had also formed relationships with members of her church. Much to her amazement, she had not seen any evidence of homesickness in her daughter, especially at Christmas. Things had all seemed to fall into place as she had hoped they would.

After the initial shock at the long snow fall and intense cold of the winter months, Charlotte felt happier than she thought she would ever be. She was comfortable at home with her family and she had formed some friendships with some of the young people at the church. They had gotten past saying to her she was lovely — or "lavelay", as it sounded to Charlotte's ear! That had always made Charlotte laugh and at home she would repeat that to her brothers.

Charlotte had even begun to call her stepfather Dad. It had taken them both by surprise when one morning as they drove to college, in conversation she had without thinking called him Dad. Realising this, James said, "I like the sound of that."

Smiling, Charlotte replied, "Me too."

As she sat at her desk that morning preparing for her lecture, Charlotte took out her diary and quickly jotted down, "The most unbelievable thing just happened. I called James Dad!" Dating and underlining what she had written she closed the diary, smiling to herself and wondering what Marcia would say when she next wrote that to her.

CHAPTER 12

NEWS FROM THE ISLAND

Happy and at peace with herself and every-one around her, Charlotte could hardly believe how quickly the last few years had passed. She had successfully completed her A levels and gone on to university to study medicine.

Having been separated from her mother for so many years, Charlotte had chosen a universi-ty as near to home as possible, since she did not want to be living away from home. However, she was persuaded by her mother and stepfather that she should at least spend her first year on the uni-versity campus. She agreed to remain on campus but would make regular visits home. Now in her fourth year of studying medicine, Charlotte be-gan to think about what she would choose for her specialist area of medicine and where she would go for her electives.

In many of her letters to Marcia, Charlotte would open up about her hopes for her future. She had toyed with the idea of studying tropical medicines and would perhaps look to Africa as her first choice for her electives or perhaps coming back to the Caribbean, and in particular to the Island where she grew up. Marcia would prompt her to return home for her electives saying that it would be so cool to have Charlotte home again. She missed Charlotte so much and all the more since Marcia and Brian had ended their relationship.

Charlotte had maintained frequent contact with her family on the Island and especially so with Marcia, whose letters were full of fun and things that made her laugh. They were also loaded with news of things happening on the Island and Charlotte looked forward to receiving her letters.

It seemed to her that in the six years since she had left the Island, so much had taken place. Her aunt no longer went to work at the cook shop in the city due to her problems with high blood pressure. She had found the problem with transport and getting to and from work on time too stressful.

On top of that Uncle Alfred, Aunt Maisie's husband, had returned home following an amputation of one of his legs. According to Marcia, her mother's decision to give up work was more to do with her "no good father" coming home again than anything to do with her mother's blood pressure. Marcia had written that this time he had come home to roost. No longer was he able to play the village rooster chasing every hen in the neighbourhood.

Marcia also sent news that with the help of her "no good father," Charlie had managed to rig up a one door lean-to shop at the back of the house. This enabled her mother to sell her special homemade coconut sweet bread and confectionaries like sugar cakes, glassies, and peppermint balls, which were a hit with the school children as they passed the shop on their way to school. She also managed to sell a few essential food items.

Marcia called it the gossip shop since it was where some of the village women gathered to exchange gossip. On occasions when any of the women who came by the shop window in the evening for gossip, they would remark to Aunt Maisie that she was silly to take her husband back. Aunt Maisie would let them know in no uncertain terms it was none of their business. She would always maintain that she had made a vow for better or for worse and that where the heart is, there is home. She was his heart and this was his home.

Marcia wrote that Charlie had moved out of the family home and was now living with his girlfriend. Since Aunt Maisie did not have him around to argue and banter with, Yvonne had taken his place. Unlike Marcia who would always prefer not to argue with her mother, Yvonne ruled the house. She was a bolshie teenager who thought she knew better than everyone in the house how everything should be done.

On occasions when embarrassed by her father (who constantly insisted on hobbling around the district with crutches on his one leg, with his pants leg folded up on the stump of his amputation instead of wearing his prosthesis), Yvonne would nag him to put on the prosthesis. On hearing her nagging at her father, Aunt Maisie would shout to Yvonne, "Show some respect and leave the man alone. If the man don't want to wear a false leg is that any business of yours?"

At which Yvonne would retort, "It's not a false leg. It's a prosthesis."

"Prostetis my eye. God gave us two hands and two feet, not two prostetis."

Aunt Maisie would shout back and the argument would go back and forth for ages while her dad would just sit laughing as the debate went on.

In one of Marcia's letters, she had told Charlotte that the Island had become independent and the government had made many changes to transport and education. Children like her sister Yvonne were now able to attend high school for free.

In other news, she explained that the young Evans had relocated to the U.S. taking Sam and Tilly and leaving old Pa Evans on his own with Walley. The old man had in the last few years found it difficult to keep the plantation running and he had begun to sell off a number of plots of land. New houses were being built on the estate. Walley occasionally came by and hung out at Aunt Maisie's shop. According to Marcia, he told Aunt Maisie he was not sure how much longer Pa Evans was going to be able hold on to what was left of the plantation. He was never the same since his wife passed away and now even more pitiful since Sam, Tilly, and their parents left for America.

One afternoon, Charlotte sat with her

parents eager to read the latest letter she had just received from Marcia. As she opened the letter, she wondered what the latest news from Marcia was going to be. She continued to read, chuckling at some of what Marcia had written. Her mother standing at the kitchen sink asked what was so funny.

Charlotte continued to read the letter and remarked that old Pa Evans had passed away.

"No!" came a cry from her mother.

Charlotte thought she saw a look of distress in her mother as she leaned forward at the sink. "What is the matter Mum?" Was she right, did the news of Pa Evans' passing affect her mother so as to cause her distress?

She saw that her mother had begun to cry. James sitting across from Charlotte moved to where Amanda was standing at the sink. He gently drew her to him and burying her head in his chest, she sobbed.

Charlotte, startled by this reaction, asked what was going on. Moving Amanda to the nearest chair, James sat her mother down. A little confused, Charlotte said, "I don't mean to be callous but what is the big deal? It is not as if he was family or you knew him that well."

Suddenly, the picture of her as a little child that had been on the Evans' sideboard flashed before her eyes. Before she had had time to think she asked,

"Was Mr, Evans my father?"

"No Charlotte," her mother said, "he was mine."

CHAPTER 13

MA BECKLES

Reeling from the shock of what her mother had just revealed, stuttering Charlotte asked, "What? How?"

Before she could ask any further questions, James, standing behind Amanda with his hands on her shoulders, said, "I think it is about time you told her the truth."

"What truth?" Charlotte said.

"Just listen," James told her. "This isn't going to be easy for either of you. Would you like me to go Mum so you two can talk?"

"No! Stay please," Amanda said. And so she began the revelation of the story of her youth and Charlotte's beginnings.

"I was sixteen and preparing for my CXE exams and my parents were nearing the completion of a transaction to buy the Big House plantation. The Evans family had lived all their lives in St. John. My father, Mr. Evans, had inherited a few small plots of land around the parish and had managed to employ field hands to help him work the few acres of land. He was well respected by the locals who called him 'Boss.'

Not only was he respected by the workers, he was also able to associate with a few of the more well-to-do people on the Island. He was a member of the Masonic Lodge and the Bridge Club and he had a few close friends in the government. In spite of this, my father didn't trust some of the people he associated with. He always had the suspicion that behind his back, they only saw him as another uneducated 'ecky becky' who was trying to move into the Island's middle and upper class circles.

He had often heard such snide remarks from the British and some Americans who had become resident on the Island, who would always say to him, 'We don't mean you, you are different.'

Percy Evans never trusted their so-called acceptance. His one ambition in life was to prove that he was equally as good as they were. He would raise himself and his family above their current status.

With this in mind, when he heard that the plantation in the city was up for sale, he jumped at the opportunity to buy it. Using what savings he had along with money he obtained from the sale of his small holdings, he purchased the plantation.

Although my father loved both of his children, I was his pride and joy and I was often told by others that he spoilt me. With pride, joy and laughter in his eyes he would deny it.

My parents were a joyful couple and lived happily with their two children, me and my brother Reginald. While Daddy was the ambitious one, my mother stayed quietly in the background, offering advice and support and making sure we were properly taken care of and educated.

Daddy was a very proud man and he was overjoyed at the prospect of owning the small plantation. Weeks of preparation and meetings with his lawyer and good friend, Alex Chambers, had gone into the transaction with one last piece of paperwork to be completed.

On the day the last piece of paper was to be signed, Daddy had asked Alex if he would be so kind as to bring the paperwork up to his house and on his way he could collect me from school. His office was not many miles from the school.

I had known Alex Chambers since I was in primary school and I had always respectfully re-ferred to him as Uncle Alex. Before leaving for school that day, my parents reminded me to wait for Uncle Alex at the school gate and be sure not to keep him waiting.

As soon as school ended, I positioned myself at the school gate. Uncle Alex drove up shortly afterwards and beckoned me to come to the car. As I got in, he asked me if I had been waiting long. He had just come from court and had not expected it to take so long. He then told me that he had left the papers he needed to take to Daddy in his office and he needed to drop by his office to collect them.

When we reached the office, he told me to come in while he collected the papers and that it would only take a couple of minutes. His associate and secretary had already left the office. We entered the office and he showed me to a room with a large couch and a bookcase. He said the evening was so hot and asked me if I wanted a glass of lemonade. I politely accepted and he left the room, returning with two glasses of lemonade.

Handing me one glass and resting the other on a small table beside the couch, he sat down beside me. As he did so, he began to play with my hair telling me how pretty I was and asking if I had a boyfriend.

Feeling uncomfortable, I asked if we could go now, by which time he had put his glass down. Placing his hand on my knee he began to move his hands up my legs. Pushing his hands away and moving as far from him as he would allow me, I continued to beg him to stop.

Although I continued to struggle, he pushed me on to my back on the couch. Struggling and pleading with him not to do what he was doing, I felt him tugging at my underwear. I realised that he was about to rape me.

Petrified and not able to free myself, I remembered reading somewhere that struggling with an abuser gave them a sense of power. I wrestled in my mind what I should do: if I stayed quiet, would he think I was happy with what he was doing? If I struggled, would it give him more power over me? As these thoughts raced through my mind, Uncle Alex took complete possession of my body and using the most foul language I had ever heard. He satisfied himself then he rolled away from me.

Crying, I got up from the couch. Picking up the small bag I had taken into the office with me[, I tidied myself as best I could and began to walk towards the door]. At this Uncle Alex told me I was not to mention what just happened to anyone and if I dared to, he would deny it. He said, as a matter of fact, no one would take my word against his.

Leaving as quickly as I could, I caught the bus heading in the direction of the bus terminal where I normally took the bus home. Getting on the bus, I wondered if there were any signs on me that indicated what had just happened to me.

With only a few stops to the terminal, I quickly got off the bus and made my way to where I would board the bus home. Thankful that the bus was already there with only a few people in the queue, I waited my turn to get on. As I did so an elderly woman beckoned me to the window seat.

Grateful that I was able to sit with my face looking out of the window and keep my tear-stained face away from the eyes of other passengers, I moved to the window seat. The elderly woman began a conversation but as I did not respond she soon gave up. I drew a book from my bag and pretended to read to avoid any further conversation with the woman.

As I stared out of the bus window, I tried to blank from my mind what Uncle Alex had done to me. At the same time, I wondered what I was going to tell my parents and what reason I would give for not coming home with Uncle Alex.

As I approached our house, I saw Alex's car parked on the outside. I knew that he would be with Daddy but could not imagine what excuse he would have given for not bringing me home.

To avoid any contact with Uncle Alex, I

entered the house by the back door instead of at the side which was my normal practice. As I did so my mother told me that Uncle Alex said he missed me by seconds as he was late but on arriving at the school gate, he saw me drive off in a car. Thinking I must have given up on his coming to pick me up, Uncle Alex assumed I had taken a lift to the bus stand. He had driven to where he thought I might alight from the car he saw me drive away in, but he could not see me, so he decided to come to the house as planned.

I thought my mother looked a bit cross as she asked why I didn't wait for Uncle Alex but because I did not respond or give any further information, she let the matter rest. Throwing my bag down on the chair nearest to the door, I headed for the shower exclaiming that I was very hot and tired.

As I showered, I could not wash the smell of Alex Chambers away nor could I erase from my mind the words he had used as he abused me. I stood under the shower until the knocking on the bathroom door and my mother called to say the meal was on the table and I had better hurry up.

During our evening meal my father repeated the story my mother had given about why I had missed meeting Uncle Alex at the school gate. I neither denied nor confirmed the story he had given my parents.

Half eating my food, I excused myself from the table, saying I had a headache and as I needed to do some study for an exam in the morning I was going for a lie down. Accepting my excuse, my parents continued chatting. My mother later told me that the topic of their conversation that night was around the transaction for the purchase of the plantation close to the city.

My father had informed my mother that within a matter of weeks they would be the sole owners of the plantation and that only one other document needed to be signed and witnessed. He told her that Alex had informed him the previous owners had now left the Island and had gone back to England, leaving their lawyers to tie up loose ends.

My mother, Evelyn, smiled and praised her husband for the excellent way he had managed to get things moving and how smoothly things had gone. My brother had been listening to the conversation between my parents and also congratulated my dad saying,

"Well done Daddy, I can't wait to leave this area. I'm sick and tired of being called 'ecky becky' and 'poor white.'"

Rising from his chair at the table my father touched him on his shoulder saying, "You and me both son."

Amanda continued recounting the story to Charlotte. Amanda had spent a restless night wondering what excuse she could give for not wanting to go to school. She felt sure she would not be able to face anyone at school, and she did not want to wonder the streets as she was aware some children did.

As the time drew near for her to leave for school, Amanda told her mother she would not be needing to prepare any lunch for her because those getting ready for their exams were given home study periods to prepare. No questions asked, Amanda stayed in her room for most of the day.

As the days went by, Amanda knew that she would not be able to keep up the pretence and she would have to face going back to school. Plucking up the courage, Amanda returned to school but her previous enthusiasm and drive to excel in the subjects she had selected waned. She felt herself no longer interested in anything and she had become moody, often snapping at her brother and dismissing her parents as they tried to communicate with her. Amanda knew she was acting out of character but felt herself helpless to control her behaviour.

Waking up one morning with a severe feeling of nausea, she wondered what could have been the cause. When for almost a week in succession, the feeling of nausea persisted it dawned on Amanda that her time of the month was also late. The thought that she might be pregnant made her feel even worse.

She rose from her bed making her way to the bathroom to vomit. She staggered as she did so. Gripping the vanity beside her bed she made it to the bathroom just in time. Holding her head over the sink and after retching several times, she returned to her room.

Gripped by fear, Amanda curled up on the bed not knowing what to do. At the sound of a knock on the door, she heard her mother's voice asking if she was ok and if she could come in. Before Amanda could reply the feeling of nausea rose in her stomach once more. Opening the door and moving past her mother she hurried to the bathroom, her mother following closely behind her.

"What's wrong Amanda, are you ill?" her mother asked.

With her head bent over the sink and with

the sound of retching, her mother asked if she should get her to the hospital. Anxiously Amanda replied, "No, I will be okay in a minute."

Following her daughter back to her room, with a look of concern, Evelyn Evans asked Amanda how long she had been feeling unwell as she thought she had heard her retching earlier. Curling up on the bed once more with her back towards her mother, Amanda said,

"I think I might be pregnant, Mother."

Not sure that she had heard her daughter correctly, Mrs. Evans asked

"What dear?"

"I think I might be pregnant Mother," Amanda repeated.

Mrs. Evans knew that Amanda had to be serious, since she only ever addressed her as Mother when she was troubled about something or was in a mood to tease her. Looking at Amanda in stunned silence, her mother asked, "What? How? Who? I didn't know you were seeing someone. How could you be pregnant you never leave the house except for school or with me and Daddy."

"I was raped Mother, by Uncle Alex. It was on the day he was asked to pick me up from school. He lied that he had missed seeing me at the school gate."

Amanda proceeded to tell her mother the whole account of what had taken place that day at Alex Chambers' law office, unburdening herself and giving words to what had happened for the first time.

"Afterwards, he threatened me that if I told anyone it was him, he would deny it. He said he would also make it difficult for Daddy to buy the plantation and that no one would take my word against his."

Numb, Mrs. Evans stared at Amanda as she remained sitting beside her on the bed. "You do believe me don't you, Mother?"

"I don't know what to believe. Why didn't you tell us when you came home?"

"What difference would it have made? The deed was done and it would have affected Daddy buying the plantation."

"The plantation! The plantation! What's more important? I need to speak to your father."

"Not yet, Mother, please. Let Daddy complete the purchase first."

Amanda had not thought beyond her father's desire to own the plantation. Amanda felt sure that confronting Alex at this stage would adversely affect her father's chances of owning the plantation. "No, Amanda, it has to be now."

Leaving Amanda's bedroom, Mrs. Evans walked back to the sitting room and made herself ready to face the day. She knew that her husband would be meeting with Alex Chambers later in the week to sign the final documents.

At breakfast, she mulled over the idea of telling him then but looking at Amanda and seeing the wane look on her face, she decided to wait until Amanda had left for school.

Throughout the day Evelyn Evans thought of all the ways she would approach the subject of Amanda being raped be Alex Chambers. To her husband, it would be unthinkable. She had to find a way to get it through to him that their daughter was telling the truth and a way to confront Alex, no matter the outcome. As the day rolled on, the opportunity seemed to be slipping by. Maybe she would broach the subject at the evening meal when they were all together and Amanda could explain and defend herself.

At six o clock, Mrs. Evans always said grace at the main meal. It was a practice Evelyn had seen in her home growing up, before her marriage to Percy. As usual Percy enquired of Reginald and Amanda how their day had gone and he quickly followed this by raising again the subject of the completion of his purchase of the plantation. This was followed by Reginald's enthusiasm at the prospect of moving away from the country to the town.

As the meal progressed, Percy thought he sensed an uneasiness in his wife and daughter. Thinking it was something to do with their imminent move from their familiar surroundings, he asked if they were bothered about the move. He assured them that it would be fine and that they would soon get used to living in the city.

Percy raised all the advantages living in the city would bring, especially for Evelyn who would find it easier to attend the hospital for her condition. For some months, Evelyn had been attending the hospital for her "condition," a word used but never really expanded upon in the presence of the children. Whatever her ailment, it was not named, it was simply spoken of as her "condition."

Evelyn had always insisted upon it being so whilst the children were at the peak of their education, as she wanted nothing to distract or stress them. She knew and prayed that she would find the right time to discuss the problem of her health with the children. It took much persuasion to get Percy to agree with her, but he eventually did.

Mustering all the courage she could find and praying that her husband would be calm and rational as they decided how to deal with the problem of Amanda's rape and pregnancy, Evelyn began by saying that there was a serious matter she wanted to discuss with the family and she wanted them to listen calmly to what she had to say. Suddenly the colour drained from Percy's face as he assumed the matter was in relation to Evelyn's health.

Amanda immediately knew what her mother wanted to discuss and looking at her mother she shouted. "No Mother!"

On hearing this, Percy was surprised that Evelyn had gone back on her word and discussed her condition with the children without informing him. Immediately he began, "I thought we agreed to wait until the children finished their exams to tell them about your condition Evelyn?"

"No, please listen to what I have to say, Percy. This is not about me."

Turning towards her husband she said,

"It is about Amanda. The news is not good. Amanda is pregnant."

With that, Percy shouted, "What nonsense! This can't be true."

"I'm afraid so. She was raped by Alex Chambers on the evening he was meant to pick her up from school."

"What?! I don't believe a word of this. Didn't Alex tell us he saw her drive off in a car as he arrived to pick her up? To involve a decent man like Alex in such a thing is ridiculous. When could Alex have raped her and why would he want to do such a thing? He's a responsible married man."

Evelyn pleaded with him to listen so she

could tell him the whole story. Beginning with the day they had asked Alex to pick Amanda up from school, she told him Alex's excuse for not seeing Amanda at the school gate had been a lie.

Percy refused to listen. As her mother continued, Amanda rose from her seat at the table and began to move towards her room. Her mother followed her bringing her back so she could explain what happened and at least defend herself. Standing next to the table across from her father, he shouted at her,

"Shut your filthy, lying mouth! Is this how I spend my money, to educate a whore?!"

In his anger, he rose from his chair and attempting to lash out at Amanda swung his open palm towards her. In a flash, Evelyn moved. With her back towards Amanda and facing Percy, she intercepted the hand moving towards Amanda, the blow accidentally landing across Evelyn's chest. She winced and groaned as the blow struck but she made no complaint.

Turning to face her mother, Amanda buried her head in her mother's chest. "Mummy he hit you."

"Never mind that, leave your father to me."

Grabbing his floppy khaki hat he had earlier placed on the back of the chair, Percy walked towards the back door, insisting he wanted Amanda out of the house and he did not want to find her there when he returned. As Percy walked through the door, Evelyn told Amanda to go to her room while she figured something out. Evelyn had always been able to get through to Percy when things were difficult and needed sorting out. She was confident that this time would be no different.

Jumping into the old Dodge jalopy, Percy drove through the gap between two cane fields. He could not stop himself repeating the words, "How could she? How could she?"

Anger and disappointment getting the better of him, Percy stopped the jalopy. He tried to make sense of what had happened at the house only moments ago and what he was hearing about the daughter he had idolised, pampered, and, according to many, spoilt. But he was also grappling with the fact that in the heat of the moment, he had struck his beloved wife. Never in all the time they had been together had he lost his temper with her or with the children. There was never any form of violence in the family. This was one thing Percy had always been proud of. In times of difficulty, he and Evelyn had always been able to figure things out.

On top of hearing Amanda's story that she had apparently been raped by someone he trusted, Percy had allowed his anger to get the better of him. Unable to contain his feelings of anger and disappointment, he gave way to uncontrollable tears and leaned into the steering wheel. He did not realise or pay any attention to the fact that he was pressing the horn of the vehicle. Not until he heard the barking of Rusty the dog did he lift his head and see the dog and Walley walking towards him.

As quickly as he could, Percy drew his handkerchief from his pocket. Drying his tears, he heard Walley shouting, "Are you okay, Boss? Is something wrong?"

"I'm okay, Walley. I think old Betsy here is playing up again," came Percy's reply.

"Want me to take a look at her, Boss?"

"No, Walley, I think she'll get going in a minute. You get going or you'll be late for your game with the fellas."

It was Walley's custom at the end of the day to sit with the other elderly men of the village under the big tamarind tree next to the local rum shop. They would have a game of dominoes before the darkness of the evening closed in. Being assured by Percy that he would be okay, Walley and Rusty the dog continued their journey along the dirt track between the two cane fields.

Feeling more composed than he had before he was interrupted by Rusty and Walley, Percy lingered a while longer to think through his plan of action for when he returned home. He decided that he would not approach Alex Chambers about the claim that he had raped Amanda, and he would forbid Evelyn from doing so also. Amanda had made her bed now she must lie in it. After all, didn't Alex say on the evening he was to pick her up from school that he had seen her go off in a car? How could they be sure Amanda was not deceiving them? He had come too close to fulfilling his dream of owning a plantation to let the reckless behaviour of a thoughtless teenager shatter his dreams. No, she had to go.

Revving up the old Dodge, he drove off making his way back to the house. As Percy entered, he saw Evelyn sitting at the dining table alone.

"Where you been, Percy? We need to talk."

"Not now, I'm exhausted," Percy replied as he walked towards the door of the room where he kept his documents in an old desk. Evelyn followed him.

"Percy, this is no way to handle the situation. I know you're disappointed, but Amanda is our daughter and her welfare comes first. We must speak to Alex about what he has done. We can't just let him get away with it."

"No, not at all. I forbid you speaking to Alex about this. Alex was clear he had seen Amanda go off in a car that evening. And what about Reggie? Have you given a thought to how this is scandal would affect him and his future?"

"My God, Percy! I never thought you would abandon your daughter for thirty pieces of silver. Is ownership of a plantation worth more than your flesh and blood?"

Evelyn left the room with tears in her eyes. Turning back towards him she said, "Amanda stays here tonight. Tomorrow I'll make arrangements for her."

As Evelyn left the room, the thought came to her that she might contact Ma Beckles to seek her help in temporarily assisting Amanda. She had known and trusted Ma Beckles for years when she lived in their area. Ma Beckles had often assisted Evelyn with the cooking and washing and caring for the children, especially during the early months of her condition. Picking up the phone, Evelyn dialled the number of Ma Beckles's neighbour asking if she could she get an urgent message to Mrs Beckles: "Please ask her to call Evelyn Evans."

Ivy Beckles knew that it had to be important and urgent to be getting a call so late from Mrs. Evans. Hurrying to her neighbour's house, she returned the call to Mrs Evans. Without much detail, Mrs. Evans asked if it was okay for Ma Beckles to accommodate Amanda for a little while. Thinking Mrs. Evans' condition had deteriorated, she said she was only too glad to help and offered to come to St. John to help her. After being reassured that that Mrs Evans was fine and told she would be given more details in the morning, both women hung up.

Percy moved towards the cupboard over the desk and drew from it a half-filled bottle of Doorly's Macaw rum. Pouring a shot of the rum, he took one long gulp and sat himself down in the chair beside the old desk. As the hours passed, he knew that he should go to bed but not wanting to face Evelyn or any further discussion, he waited until he thought she was asleep.

Percy knew in his heart that he should have at least apologised for lashing out at Amanda and accidentally hitting his wife, but his pride prevented him from doing so. His one purpose was to secure ownership of the plantation and nothing was going to get in his way. To apologise would make him seem weak and give the impression that he had recanted.

Percy quietly undressed for bed and climbed in beside his wife. He knew that she was not asleep but neither spoke a word. Rising early in the morning and hoping not to have to face either his wife or Amanda, Percy made himself a cup of tea. On leaving the house, he made his way out to one of the fields.

Evelyn heard the click of the door and knew that her husband had left the house. Reaching for her dressing gown, she made her way to Amanda's room telling her to get up and get herself ready as they were going into town. Evelyn knocked on

Reggie's door calling to him to get up and make his breakfast and lunch before going to school. Mumbling, "Ok, Mummy," Reggie turned over and stayed in bed. Remembering the conversation that had gone on at the dinner table the night before, he had no inclination to face the family, especially his sister.

After taking a shower and getting herself dressed, Evelyn returned to Amanda's room. She told Amanda to pack a few items of clothing because she was taking her to town to stay with Ma Beckles for a little while, until her father had calmed down and they had figured out what to do about Alex and the pregnancy.

"What about school?" Amanda asked.

"We will figure that out later too," her mother replied.

As they spoke, Amanda could feel nausea rising in her stomach and hurried to the bathroom. Mrs. Evans could see that her daughter was about to be sick. Making her way to the kitchen, Evelyn made Amanda a cup of ginger tea in the hope that it would settle Amanda's stomach long enough for them to get to Ma Beckles in town.

Leaving Amanda with the tea, Mrs. Evans went to the outhouse in the yard and knocked on the door. She called to Walley to make himself ready. She needed him to drive her and Amanda to town. "Yes Mistress," came the reply. "Ready in two ticks."

Percy slowly took a walk through the rows of sugar cane and came to the plot of land growing potatoes. He saw two of the workers weeding. Catching sight of him they shouted, "Morning Boss. You out early."

Not wanting to have too much of a conversation, he returned the greeting and walked on. He carried on walking to the end of the potato plot and thinking it he should be getting back, he took from his pocket the watch hanging from a chain attached to his belt: almost 8:30. He thought if he took the walk back slowly, maybe his wife and daughter would have left the house.

Nearing the house he saw the family car still parked by the side of the house and he knew they were still at home. Mustering enough courage to face them, he entered the house. He met his wife standing at the dining table and once again she pleaded with him to change his mind and allow Amanda to remain at home. Percy was adamant and resolute. She had to go.

Moving towards the spare room where he kept his documents in the old desk, Percy sat in the chair placing one hand on his head whilst resting his elbow on the desk. Percy convinced himself he had made the right decision. He had come too far to let anything or anyone—even his much-loved daughter—stand in the way of his dream of being a plantation owner.

His one thought was raising the status of his family and showing the "newbies" at the Lodge and Bridge Club that he was as good as they were. He was tired of the snide remarks about 'ecky beckies' and 'St. John whites.' He would show them that even though the colour of his skin looked a bit rusty from outdoor work and the sun, he was as much a Caucasian as they were. After all, his great grandparents had been white Irish. It was also one of his dreams that he would one day search for his Irish roots. These thoughts filled his mind as he waited for his wife and daughter to leave the house.

Seeing the half open door and her father sitting in his chair, Amanda knocked on the door and entered the room. In a trembling voice she said, "Good morning Daddy. I'm going now. I love you Daddy."

With tears streaming down her face, she left her father staring mutely into the nothingness in front of him. Her words broke his heart but he remained resolute. Amanda was devastated by her father's coldness towards her, blanking out all thoughts of the abuse by Alex. Uppermost in her mind was the loss of her relationship with her father.

Burying her face in her mother's chest, Amanda cried loudly. Steering her to the nearest chair, Evelyn approached her husband, once more pleading with him to change his mind. Percy remained silent. As she left the room, she could not remember ever feeling so helpless and alone. In all the years she had been married to Percy, there was never a time that they had not been able to settle their differences and make compromises. They had always been able to talk things through and settle them amicably. His current attitude saddened her.

Picking up the small suitcase from beside the chair, Evelyn motioned to Amanda to follow her to the car where Walley had been waiting. Evelyn sat in the front seat of the car. She knew that at some point she would have to give Walley some reason why they were taking Amanda to Ma Beckles. She knew he could be trusted and would not gossip but for now, she would tell him only as much as he needed to know.

Content with this idea, she allowed her thoughts to return to Amanda and Ma Beckles. Glancing occasionally at Amanda sitting in the back of the car, Evelyn could see the pain and distress of the situation in her daughter's face and it pained her. Silently she prayed for strength and wisdom to deal with this trial. Uppermost in her mind was staying in good enough health to support Amanda and see the child she was carrying. The circumstances of its conception were not ideal, but it would be her flesh and blood and she would not deny it.

They pulled up outside Ma Beckles' house. Amanda could feel her stomach turning and this time it was not from the pregnancy but from fear and shame. She had known Ma Beckles all her life, but never in her wildest dreams did she ever imagine that she would spend a night in her house, let alone having to live with her, no matter how temporary.

Amanda knew that Ma Beckles had two adult children: a son who worked at the docks and a daughter married with a young son and pregnant with another. Her mother had filled her in with the Beckles' family situation and condition of the Beckles' home. She had assured Amanda that within a week or two her father would have seen sense and calmed down and she would be able to return home.

Ma Beckles was waiting outside as they drew up. She welcomed them warmly, waving to Walley who waited outside in the car. Entering the house, they could see Maisie Brown, Ma Beckles' daughter, sitting at the table feeding her two-year-old son. Mrs. Evans called a greeting to Maisie and asked how she and her son were. Maisie smiled and waved back and carried on feeding her son. Ma Beckles coaxed the child to come over to say hello but his mother kept hold of him.

Turning to Mrs. Evans and Amanda, Ma Beckles asked Amanda how she was and suggested to them to follow her to the room that Amanda would use. She said it had been her son's room but since he had left for one of the other islands months ago and no one had heard from him, the room had been unoccupied. She continued that it was a bit small but should be ample for Amanda as she was sure her daddy would be missing her and wanting her home soon. And as she always said, "Where there is room in the heart, there is room in the home."

So far, Ma Beckles did not know the reason for Amanda being sent from home, neither did she press for any details. She knew that Evelyn trusted her and in time she would confide in her. As Amanda and her mother sat on the bed, Ma Beckles told them she was in no doubt that before the week was out Mr. Evans would come to get her himself. She had seen with her own two eyes how he doted on his daughter and the love and care he felt for his family.

While Amanda listened to the old woman, she thought how true that might have been in the past. But judging from the anger she had seen in her father's face and the abusive language he had used to describe her last night after the disclosure, she was not sure what the old woman was saying was true any longer.

Ma Beckles talked about her family and she said that Maisie was a bit moody at times, but given that she was pregnant and also dealing with a two year old, it was expected. Other than that, she was okay.

Continuing their conversation, Mrs Evans handed Ma Beckles an envelope telling her it was some money to assist her with food for Amanda. Ma Beckles pushed her hand away and refused to take the money on account that it would not be long before Amanda was home where she belonged. The matter of the money concluded with Mrs. Evans persuading Ma Beckles to take the money. Having done so, Mrs. Evans and Amanda followed Ma Beckles outside to have a look around.

As they did so, they walked through the kitchen bumping into Maisie carrying her son in her arms. Reaching out, Mrs. Evans stroked the child's head asking his name. Half smiling, Maisie said it was Charlie. The child shyly turned his head into his mother's bosom. As he did so, Mrs. Evans tapped Maisie on her belly asking her when was the next baby due. Maisie replied, "In another six months."

"A while to go yet," Mrs. Evans said. With that, she followed Ma Beckles and Amanda out of the door.

Walking with Amanda and her mother around the house, Ma Beckles pointed out landmarks and drew their attention to the plantation's Big House nestled amongst the trees in the far distance. Evelyn Evans' heart sank as she realised it was the house and plantation they would be moving to in a few months. She hoped in her heart that her husband would change his mind and have their daughter home and Amanda and her child would have the privilege of living with them on the plantation.

While Ma Beckles continued to point out the various landmarks, Amanda asked if she could return indoors. She felt the need to communicate with Maisie since she was to be living with her temporarily. "Of course," came the reply and Amanda returned to the house.

Ma Beckles pointed to the ships she could see in the harbour. She led Mrs. Evans to the rock that stuck out near the house where at night they would sit and watch the ships anchored and lit up as they came and went from the docks. As the two women seated themselves on the rock, Mrs. Evans had the opportunity to unburden herself.

She spoke about the situation that led her to be needing help, and about her husband's belligerence. As Evelyn spoke, tears rolled down her cheeks. Drawing her close and resting her hand on Mrs. Evans' shoulder, Ma Beckles assured her that things would turn out well given time. She reminded Evelyn that she could always count on her for support and she would do whatever was needed to look after Amanda, no matter how long it was going to be.

With that, the two women returned to the house. Calling to Amanda, Mrs. Evans told her daughter she needed to be getting back home but she would call her via the neighbour before she went to bed. Hugging her daughter, she left the house and headed to the vehicle where Walley sat waiting for her.

On the journey home, Evelyn gave Walley a reason for removing her daughter from her home so abruptly. Although Walley could be trusted, until she was sure how long her husband would remain adamant that Amanda was to leave their home and they had sorted out the issue of the rape and pregnancy, she didn't tell Walley anything other than that Mr. Evans had had a serious disagreement with Amanda and it was necessary for her to be away from home until he had calmed down. She was not sure how long it was going to take the stubborn old fool to come to his senses, she told him, but for now Ma Beckles had agreed to look after Amanda. Walley made no comment at the explanation and they continued the journey back in total silence.

CHAPTER 14

MORE TRUTH

As the days rolled into weeks and weeks into months, Percy Evans remained adamant that he did not want his daughter returning home. He took the position that she had made her bed and she must now lie in it. The transactions to own the plantation had been completed and the move was imminent. Amanda, her pregnancy now apparent, was sure that there was no chance of her ever reconciling with her father and returning home to her family. Her place in the Beckles' household now seemed permanent. Amanda continued to have contact with her mother either at the home of Ma Beckles or they would meet somewhere in the city.

Having now moved to the plantation and the Big House, it pained Evelyn Evans that her daughter or the child born to her would never see the inside of the Big House or set foot on the plantation.

Amanda had not found Maisie Brown easy to get along with. When Maisie realised that Amanda's stay with the family was longer than she had expected, she became resentful and arguments with her mother often ensued. Maisie's attitude to Amanda and the quarrels with her mother appeared to increase whenever Maisie's husband disappeared. He would leave home without anyone knowing where he had gone, only to return days or weeks later to the welcoming arms of his wife.

Maisie soon gave birth to her second child, a girl. With the arrival of the baby the relationship between Maisie and Amanda seemed to improve as Amanda was on hand and ready to assist Maisie with the care of her son and the newborn.

Eight months after moving to the Beckles' household, with her mother present, Amanda gave birth to a baby girl whom she later named Charlotte Evangeline Beckles. Having had no contact with her father in months and knowing that he no longer considered her a part of his family, Amanda and her mother had sought Ma Beckles' permission to use the Beckles family name for her child.

With two small children just months apart and a two-year-old in the Beckles household, Ma Beckles was kept busy. Tensions often ran high between Maisie and Ma Beckles, who would often accuse her mother of giving more attention to people that were not her own flesh and blood. These tensions and arguments continued as Amanda came to grips with being a teenage mum. She would many times find herself in tears at Maisie's remarks and moods.

By the time Charlotte reached her first birthday, Mrs. Evans and Ma Beckles agreed that it was time for Amanda to return to school to complete her CXEs or at least to some form of education. With financial help from Mrs. Evans, Ma Beckles would care for Charlotte. Amanda being reluctant to return to school opted for private tuition to complete her CXEs.

Evelyn Evans continued to press her husband to have Amanda and Charlotte come home, but the more she pressed him, the more he dug his heels in. He refused to acknowledge his daughter or her child as a part of his family. During the months that Amanda was estranged from her family, the relationship between Percy and his wife, which had once been harmonious and strong, had greatly deteriorated. They had become more distant as the days went by. However, Percy was conscious of his wife's ill health, and he could see physical changes in her posture and demeanour.

Time had not diminished the demons inside of him in relation to Amanda and what he called her "accusation" of Alex Chambers raping her. Even though for some time he had noticed a cooling off in the relationship between himself and Alex Chambers, he had put it down to the transaction for the purchase of the plantation being at an end.

Try as he might, he could not allow himself to believe that Alex had raped his daughter. To Percy, Alex was a fine outstanding young man, a lawyer, and after all, Alex's father was an MP. Blinded by these thoughts Percy had disowned his daughter. Driven by pride, guilt, and a desire to move up the social ladder, Percy watched the disintegration of his family. He looked for ways to relieve the physical pressure on Evelyn to maintain the home, employing domestic help for her. Whether it was out of concern for his wife whom he watched grow smaller and smaller in stature every day with no real zest for life, or for the sake of his new status as a plantation owner, it was hard to tell.

Grateful for the help in the home, Evelyn found more time to spend with Amanda and Charlotte. Amanda had by this time successfully completed her CXE exams and was training as a secretary. With the help of her mother and Ma Beckles, Amanda felt confident that it was time for her to move out of the Beckles' family home and make it on her own as a young mum. She consulted with her mother and Ma Beckles who agreed that it might be good for her. As long as she did not move too far away, they would continue to support her practically and financially.

Just as Amanda had been taught as a child to address all close adult male relatives and friends as 'uncle' or 'grandpa' and adult female relatives and friends as 'aunty' or 'grandma,' she had taught this to Charlotte. So by the time Charlotte was three years old, she had known Evelyn Evans as 'Grandma', and never as Mrs. Evans.

Amanda settled in her role as single mother to her daughter Charlotte. She enjoyed her work as a secretary but felt there was something more and better she wanted to do. She was fortunate to have Ma Beckles care for Charlotte during the week whilst she worked. She also continued to have some financial support from her mother. Amanda continued her Saturday meet ups in town with her mother, taking Charlotte along with her. Charlotte would always refer to Evelyn as "the nice lady grandma" who bought her ice cream when they went to town.

One Saturday, before Amanda's planned meeting with her mother, Evelyn had sent a message to cancel their meeting. She did not give any reason but promised that she would meet with Amanda the following week. On Thursday of the following week, Amanda received a letter from her mother in which she wrote that she was not well and that she had not been well for a long time. Evelyn explained that she had been hoping to discuss her illness with Amanda and Reginald once they had finished their exams, but the unfortunate situation which caused Amanda to be separated from the family had delayed her telling them.

In the letter Evelyn explained as best she could, that the condition of her illness had worsened and she would be needing a period of hospitalization. She advised to Amanda that to avoid any confrontation with her father she would arrange for her to visit at the hospital at a time when her father was not doing so.

Amanda recounted how she had become distraught at the news and, as always, sought the comfort and advice of Ma Beckles. It was then that Ma Beckles had suggested to her that it might be a good idea to write to her mother before she went into the hospital and after she returned. In the meantime, Amanda and Ma Beckles would visit when her mother went into the hospital. They also thought how they would tell Charlotte why she would not be seeing the "nice lady grandma" who bought her ice cream on Saturdays.

★★★★★

As Amanda continued to explain to Charlotte the events of the past, James could see how much distress it was causing Amanda and how it had begun to affect Charlotte. He thought it might be a good idea if the conversation continued another time. He said it might be a good time for them to have a cup of tea. Amanda was sure she wanted Charlotte to have the full story. She said she realised she had left it for far too long to tell Charlotte and it was better to get it all out in the open—for both herself and Charlotte's sake.

At no point during the revelation did Amanda condemn Alex Chambers or dwell on the incident. What distressed her most is the break-up and separation in her relationship with her father and the loss of her mother.

James said he would make the tea anyway. Whilst James was busy making them cups of tea, Amanda continued to share with Charlotte the history of their early years. She went on to tell Charlotte of Evelyn's deterioration. According to Amanda, her mother had only remained in the hospital for a period of two weeks before she returned home to the Big House.

On Evelyn's discharge from hospital, Amanda began to correspond with her mother by letter until, at a certain point, there were no further replies. She assumed that her mother's condition had worsened and she was no longer able to write. In one of Amanda's letters she had written to her mother that she was thinking of making an application to a hospital in the UK to study nursing and, if successful, she would leave the Island. She said she would leave Charlotte behind in the care of Ma Beckles until Amanda was able to send for her to join her in the UK.

Amanda explained to Charlotte that she had made a vow to herself that the rape by Alex Chambers was not going to be the end of her. She would blank it from her mind and move on. God had blessed her with her beautiful daughter and she was fully supported by a mother and grandmother-figure who loved her. She also told Charlotte that meeting and marrying James was one of the best things that had ever happened to her.

There had not been any response from her mother to the letter. She never knew if her mother ever got the chance to read the letter as within a month of her mother's return from hospital, Evelyn had passed away. She had remained the loving mother, grandma, and source of moral and financial support to Amanda and Charlotte until her illness took its toll.

As she recalled the death of her mother, Amanda broke into uncontrollable sobs. Leaving the pot of tea and the mugs on the table, James reached for Amanda. He embraced her and held her until the crying stopped. James walked Amanda to their bedroom, leaving Charlotte to process all that her mother had revealed.

CHAPTER 15

THE MORNING AFTER THE TRUTH

After they left the room, Charlotte sat alone grappling with mixed feelings of anger, shame, and confusion: confusion about her own identity; anger that all her life she had been lied to even by the people she had most trusted: her own mother and her beloved "grandmother" Ma Beckles. Did Marcia and Charlie know?

In her confusion, she told herself that the only person who had really been truthful in the whole matter was Aunt Maisie who had never hidden her feelings of resentment. Charlotte now understood some of Aunt Maisie's remarks during her quarrels with her grandmother and the things she would say, like "Oh what a tangled web we weave when first we practice to deceive," and "Whatever is done in the dark will be known in the light and shouted from the roof top."

Aunt Maisie had gone as far as telling Charlotte on the day of her grandmother's funeral that she should be glad she had a roof over her head. Charlotte remembered vividly one of the worse arguments she had overheard between Aunt Maisie and her grandmother. That day, Charlotte had followed Marcia and Charlie to the beach unaccompanied by an adult. Her grandmother had gone into the city and as the children were on their school holidays, Aunt Maisie had given them her permission to go with a group of other children to the beach.

On her grandmother's return home from the city, when she learned that Charlotte had gone with the other children, her grandmother was frantic. The quarrel began with her grandmother telling Aunt Maisie, "The sea in have no back door," and chastising Aunt Maisie for allowing Charlotte to go to the beach without an adult.

This remark gave Aunt Maisie the opportunity to remind her mother of the constant favouritism she had shown to Charlotte.

Charlotte concluded that Marcia, who was known to listen at key holes and repeat everything she heard, could not have known. She would never have been able to keep that from her, especially during all those nights when they had talked about the photo of Charlotte as a child that she'd seen on the Evans' sideboard.

Charlotte realized as her mother recounted

the story of her youth that her mind had rested solely on herself. Aware that she had not shown any sympathy or compassion over her mother's own ordeal, she regretted now that she had only thought about things from her own perspective and had not considered how much her mother had suffered.

She scolded herself for seeming so heartless. She was ashamed for, after all, it was her mother who had suffered the most. Amanda had suffered the physical attack of the sexual abuse that had not only abruptly interrupted her education, but also brought the shame of a teenage pregnancy. Worst of all, she had been disowned by her father and separated from her family only to later have to watch from afar as her mother deteriorated into nothingness from a condition that was never spoken of.

Yet now her mother's life appeared to be full of love and tranquillity. She had a loving husband and children. Charlotte's grandmother would have said, "It could only have been by the grace of God." So who was she to be angry with? Her mother for keeping the circumstances of her birth secret?

Charlotte thought she had to find a way to let her mother know how much she loved her and how much it pained her to see her mother so distressed, with no way of easing the suffering she was going through. But she did not know what approach to take. Rising from her chair with tears in her eyes she went off to bed.

After the events of the previous night, Charlotte awoke on Saturday morning. Usually the house would be quiet but Charlotte could hear her brothers running around downstairs. Her mother was calling to them to be quiet as their sister was asleep.

It seemed like only a few hours since her mother and stepfather had left her at the table following her mother's revelation. Charlotte was hesitant to get out of bed. She did not know what her reaction to her mother would be in the full light of day. She knew that the anger she felt at her mother last night had now shifted to Alex Chambers. Unconsciously she whispered, "Dear Lord, help me to cope with this situation."

Forcing herself to get out of bed, she showered and made herself ready to face the day. On reaching the kitchen, Charlotte greeted her parents and with a slight smile asked how they had slept. James replied that they had managed to sleep but they had decided that they needed to clear the air this morning and be sure that the revelations of last night had not disrupted the family dynamics.

He asked Charlotte how she was feeling about the whole matter. Charlotte replied that she was not sure how she was expected to feel as the story came as such a surprise. She said she was sorry for all that her mother had gone through and that she did not mean to seem dismissive of her suffering last night. Charlotte said if she were to be angry and resentful at anyone it would have to be at Alex Chambers and at Pa Evans for not believing her mother, but it was always the case that the blame is levelled at victims whilst perpetrators go free.

James said he understood her feelings but that was too broad a statement to make. Perpetrators did not always go free. "As Christians," he continued, "we have to have a heart of forgiveness and be able to forgive and move on." He said God had healed her mother of the wounds and given her a new life.

Charlotte said, "How easy it is for people to speak of forgiveness. Should the measure you give not be the measure you receive?"

James replied that sometimes we have to condemn the sin and not the sinner.

On hearing this, Charlotte became more angry. She remembered the long arguments she had been involved in during her A level English class on Shakespeare's *Measure for Measure*. Many times her classmates had clashed on the text "condemn the fault and not the actor of it." Was her stepfather saying that such a heinous crime should be forgiven?

Raising her tone as she often did in her English class, she quotes the character Isabella from Shakespeare's "Measure for Measure": "Oh, it is excellent to have a giant's strength, but it is tyrannous to use it like a giant."

James, being an English tutor, realised that Charlotte was thinking and speaking from a youthful academic perspective and not from a biblical viewpoint. He matched her quote with, "The miserable have no other medicine, but only hope," citing the character Claudio's words of hope of mercy and forgiveness from the same play.

James reminded Charlotte, "Scripture says that we are never to repay evil with evil and that if we are to have God's forgiveness for our own sins, then we must be ready to forgive others."

Charlotte, still angry asked, "Does that mean that every time a child or woman is raped or abused we turn a blind eye and say God forgive you?"

"Not at all," James said. "I'm simply saying that God, who is a just God, metes out punishment in his own way. In your mother's case, Alex Chambers might not have come to criminal justice but who is to say that he isn't imprisoned by guilt and torment? That could be far worse than paying a judicial penalty. The memory of his action will forever haunt him until he seeks God's forgiveness. God has given your mother beauty for ashes: she has a loving family and although the loss and separation from her family was painful, God binds up the broken hearted."

CHAPTER 16

SETTING MATTERS STRAIGHT

Within eight short years of his ownership of the plantation, Percy no longer had the kind of interest or enthusiasm he once had. The period was over, and as his late wife had said, he had sold his family for thirty pieces of silver. Percy called to mind verses of Scripture his mother had quoted after she had her "born again experience," as she called it. Both his parents had only given their lives to Christ nearing the end of their lives and his mother's favourite Scripture verse was "for what shall it profit a man to gain the whole world and loose his soul?" Percy had never really paid any heed to these words when his mother had tried to persuade him to come to church with them and to become a Christian. Percy had thought he had his whole life ahead of him and like his parents, he would do that later in life.

He had married a wonderful, caring woman, had started a family, and life could not have been any better, especially after years of dreaming of achieving greatness. He had indeed succeeded in planting a small plantation. He was running with the big boys and standing shoulder to shoulder if not above some of them.

Slumped in his chair, Percy could never have envisaged the way things would turn out: estranged from his beloved daughter, the years of coldness and emptiness between him and his wife after he evicted Amanda from their home; her deterioration of spirit and eventually her body. He had never felt so alone in his entire life as he looked back over the past years. Before her passing, Evelyn had made him promise that he would try to reconcile with Amanda. While Evelyn had been fortunate enough to have a brief relationship with Amanda's daughter, Charlotte, it had not been as meaningful as she would have liked. With tears in his eyes, Percy had made Evelyn the promise that he would. The time had now come; he could no longer put off what he had to do.

Lifting the battered valise Evelyn had kept on the shelf of her wardrobe, he placed it on the table in front of him, wondering what it would reveal. He opened it and discovered a mound of opened letters, which he knew straight away were from Amanda because he was familiar with her handwriting. Percy wondered why his wife and daughter had felt the need to correspond in writing when only a stone's throw distance had separated them from the Big House. Then it dawned on him that in the few months before his wife's passing, she had given up leaving the house. He knew that prior to her doing so she had been meeting with their daughter weekly, but it was a subject they had long since ceased to discuss.

As Percy began to read the letters, he was blinded by his tears. In each letter, Amanda had expressed her love for her father and how much she dearly loved him. It was her dearest wish that one day she round be reunited with him and also with her mother and brother, both of whom she missed very much. She had explained that her plans to go to England were finalized and she would be leaving soon to start her nursing training.

Furthermore, she had agreed to leave her daughter Charlotte with Grandma Beckles. At Charlotte's mention of Ivy Beckles as her grandmother, Percy felt remorse. He realized just how much damage his actions had caused. Not only had it deprived his beloved Evelyn of her daughter and her grandchild, it may even have hastened her demise.

Percy held his face in his hands and wept. It was the third time Percy had broken down in tears. The first had been on the evening his wife had disclosed the sexual abuse of their daughter and his refusal to accept that his friend would do such a thing. The next time had been at the death of his beloved wife and now, the third time as he read his daughter's letters to her mother.

Again and again he repeated, "How can I repair such damage?" There was only one way to start. He would contact Alex Chambers to prepare the will and he would confront him about his rape of Amanda. Yes, the damage had been done but it was not too late for a confession and reparations to Amanda and Charlotte. And what about his responsibilities to Charlotte? Percy knew what he had to do and, like Judas in the Bible, he had to do it quickly before he changed his mind. Picking up the phone, Percy dialled Alex and set up the appointment.

It was not a meeting Alex was looking forward to. He did not like the sound of Percy's voice when he called. He knew that over the years their relationship as friends had cooled. He had remained Percy's lawyer but it was not the same. At times, Alex had attributed it to Percy's inexperience at running a plantation and also the illness and death of his wife. Somehow this phone call and its urgency made him feel uneasy.

For years since his abuse of Amanda, Alex Chambers had been restless. It had even affected his relationship with his wife to the extent that it had resulted in a divorce. Alex had thought a brief period away from the Island and the practice would ease his restlessness. So he had left the practice in the hands of an associate for a few years while he went off to the University of the West Indies in Trinidad on a short course. During that time, he drifted into one relationship after another but none of them were meaningful.

Returning to the Island, he took up his law practice from where he had left off, but his restlessness continued. At times Alex thought he was losing his mind. At night he would wake up drenched in sweat, having to keep the bedroom window open to cool the room. He would imagine a faceless image staring through the window and a voice saying, "I saw what you did and I know who you are." He would get up to close the window, only to find that the noise from the window was an unlatched shutter. He consoled himself with the thought that the voice he heard was no more than a line from a film he had seen a long time ago. Closing the window, he would return to bed, hoping to catch a few more hours of uninterrupted sleep.

Not wanting to confront Alex in the same office where he had violated Amanda, Percy suggested they meet in one of the other offices of Chambers & Chambers. Thinking almost the same as Percy, Alex was relieved and happy to do so. As the two men arrived, their meeting was stiff and official, not as it had been in the past. Percy suggested getting down to the business of the writing of the will as there was another matter he wanted them to discuss.

As Alex proceeded to draw up the will, Alex asked Percy if he had remembered to bring along someone to witness the signing of the document and sure enough, Percy had brought along Walley who had been waiting outside in the car. The most important part of the will was the inheritance Percy was leaving to his daughter, Amanda. He was keeping his promise to Evelyn but more than that, he was doing it from his own free intention.

More and more over the past ten years he had had a gut feeling that his wife and daughter had been telling the truth all along and it had been his own pride and stubbornness that had blinded him, refusing to allow him to accept that truth. Today he was going to make his feelings known and confront Alex about what he had done.

Percy's inheritance to Amanda was the Big

House and the surrounding land. Other portions of the land were to go to his son and his family. He had also made some provision for Charlotte and for Walley. The business of the will out of the way, Alex said to Percy "I believe there was another matter you wanted us to discuss?"

"There is," Percy said slowly. "It has been on my mind for a very long time now but until now I have not had the courage to broach the subject. I want to ask you a question and I want an honest answer. Alex, did you rape my daughter on the day you were meant to collect her from school?"

Ashen faced and with a quivering voice Alex said "You do not know how relieved I am to finally have to confess and admit to you that in a moment of weakness I lost control of my emotions on that day. I was having a particularly bad time in my marriage and as I collected Amanda from school, she was like a breath of fresh air, innocent and beautiful. I lost control Percy, I never meant to hurt her. It was not planned."

"You expect me to accept your poor excuse for violating my daughter and destroying my family? I believed you to be a decent human being, a respectable married man. I stuck my neck out for you when my daughter and my wife disclosed it to me over twenty years ago. I trusted you Alex. You were meant to be my friend, as well as my lawyer. How could you have abused my trust? You ruined my family's life and sent my wife to her grave sooner than she should have. Have you no common decency, no shame, no remorse?

"I demand that you seek out my daughter and granddaughter and ask for their forgiveness for the pain and suffering you brought to our family.

As far as I am concerned I no longer consider you to be a friend of mine. You, you, you're an animal! But know this for sure, 'what you sow you shall reap.' You may have escaped the law which you yourself practice, but as sure as I am standing here, you will pay for what you did to my daughter and my family."

Standing to his feet and leaning on his walking stick, Percy walked to the car.

There was one other matter he had to fix. He had to write to Amanda and seek her forgiveness. He promised himself as soon as he found the courage, he would write to her. He would have Walley find out Charlotte's address, using the excuse that Sam and Tilly needed to get in touch with her. He knew Charlotte had gone to her mother in England and that she would not hesitate to send her address to Sam and Tilly.

Alex watched as Percy walked towards his car, Percy' last words echoing in his mind. He groaned at the thought of having to make contact with Amanda. After all these years, how would he find her? What would he say to her? But he knew in his heart that Percy was right. He would find Amanda and ask for her forgiveness and find a way to repair the damage he had done. It was the only way he would find peace. But what if Amanda did not want to forgive him?

Alex had not attended a church in years except for funerals and weddings. As a boy and a youth, he had attended Sunday school and had even sung in the choir. He knew all the passages of Scripture and memory verses pertaining to mercy and forgiveness. He thought maybe just this once he would attend church to find peace of mind and ways to rid him of the demons that plagued him. He would seek the answers he needed from going to church. He would make a full confession to a priest. *That's it*, he thought to himself. *They are bound to confidentiality, so no one but God and the priest will know what I had confessed.* Feeling confident that he was on the right track, he left the office and drove home.

Days later, after he had attended church and made his confession, Alex decided he would take Percy's advice and try to find a way to seek Amanda's forgiveness. It was not too late. The priest had told him it was never too late to ask for forgiveness.

CHAPTER 17

AN UNEXPECTED PATIENT

Having persuaded Walley to divulge Amanda's address in the UK, Alex prepared himself for the trip and tasks ahead. He felt confident that on meeting with Amanda he would not only lay his demons to rest, but he would obtain Amanda's forgiveness and also get to meet the daughter she had given birth to on account of his abuse. He did not want to waste any time in booking a flight and traveling to the UK, fearing that to delay meeting with Amanda he would lose his confidence in facing her again after what he had done so long ago.

Booking himself into an airport hotel on arrival until he figured out how he would go about meeting Amanda, it was uppermost in his mind how he would go about meeting her. Should he call her or should he write to her on the pretence that it was in connection with her father's will? He concluded there was no time to write to her and even if he did, would she respond? Instead, he would brave it. Using the address Walley had given him, he would find her and face the consequences.

Alex settled himself into his hotel room and firmed up his plan for how he was going to meet with Amanda. Not only did he obtain the home address of Amanda, he had also found out where she worked as a nurse. His plan was to visit the hospital and make enquiries regarding her times of duty. He had learned from Walley that she had become a nursing sister at the hospital. Most of this information Walley had gathered from Aunt Maisie on occasion when he passed the time sitting on a bench in her "gossip shop," as Marcia called it. Alex had figured that with Amanda being a prominent member of the nursing staff, it would not be difficult to locate her. He would hire a car and make his way to the hospital. He thought to himself he might not succeed in locating her on his first attempt, so having a car would make it easier should he need to try several times.

★★★★★

Arriving back at her hospital accommodation after the tempestuous night at home and the frustrating discussions she had with her stepfather, Charlotte was glad to be alone in her room after work. She thought it was where she could switch off all that was going on in her head. As she entered the room, she tossed her bag to the floor and flung herself across the bed. Trying to make sense of all that she had heard from her mother, Charlotte sobbed her heart out.

In the days that followed, Charlotte went about her work mechanically, each day eager to start work but just as eager for her shift to end. A number of times she thought of writing to Marcia and confiding in her. At other times she felt as angry with Marcia as she was with her mother and with other members of her family.

As she woke up that morning, she remembered she had promised her brothers she would take them out as it was her day off duty. Sitting on the bed and contemplating how she would face her mother and stepfather, there was a knock on her door. It was one of her colleagues asking if she could do her a favour and swap their shifts for the day. She had known from the roster that it was one of Charlotte's days off. Seizing the opportunity and without hesitation, Charlotte agreed to the swap. She was grateful that the situation had arisen as it made it easier for her to tell her family she was sorry but had to work and was sorry she would not be able to keep her promise but would make it up to them soon.

On preparing herself for her walk to the Accident and Emergency Department, the sound of her emergency bleep sounded. Throwing her white coat on and placing her stethoscope around her neck, she hurried along the corridor. On reaching Accident & Emergency, she was told that there had been a bad accident, and three persons had been brought in by ambulance under police escort. Two of the casualties were conscious and had only minor injuries and could be discharged after treatment. But the third person was barely conscious and needed intensive care treatment. The nursing staff and the police had yet to establish his identity.

Making her way to the bedside behind the drawn curtain, Charlotte asked the nurses about the critically ill patient's vital signs. As she prepared to take a closer look at the patient, she was told that he had been drifting in and out of consciousness since he was brought in. Having removed his jacket and taken his briefcase, they now established that his name was Alex Chambers and from the passport found in his jacket pocket, he had recently arrived in the country. On hearing the name, Charlotte gasped.

"What did you say his name is?" she asked.

Charlotte refused to entertain the notion that this could be the very man who only a few nights ago her mother revealed had abused her. Trying to push that idea out of her mind, she pressed on his sternum, and repeated several times, "Mr. Chambers, can you hear me? Mr. Chambers, open your eyes!"

But there was no response. Giving the orders for further treatment, including a brain scan, Charlotte walked to the nurses' station where police officers were waiting for further information. They had already interviewed the other injured couple who informed the police that they had been in their car and the other car came from nowhere and smashed into them on the wrong side of the road.

The police, with the help of the nursing staff, searched the pockets and briefcase of Alex Chambers and established that he was a lawyer and had only arrived in the UK a few days ago. He had rented a car and by the looks of it, he was on his way to a hospital not very far away and with only one other address besides the address of the hotel and car rental company. It was assumed he was going to the hospital to meet with the named person on the address.

Charlotte could not believe how fate had made that turn. In her heart she prayed silently that it was not the same Alex Chambers. Reluctant to enquire whose name was on the address found in his briefcase, she convinced herself that it was a coincidence that the patient was also named Alex Chambers.

As the patient was returned to the Emergency Department following his brain scan, his condition appeared to have deteriorated. Having examined the results of the scan and consulted with her senior colleague, Charlotte gave instructions to move Mr. Chambers to the intensive care ward. Feeling she could no longer refuse to accept that this was the Alex Chambers who had ruined the lives of her family, she decided to take a closer look at the information on his identity. Having done so she confirmed that he was and it was her mother's address he had been looking for. But how could he have gotten hold of her mother's address and also known where she worked? She was sure that it could not have come from Aunt Maisie or Charlie or even from Marcia. She came to the conclusion that it must have been from Pa Evans or from Sam and Tilly's parents before they left the Island.

Wondering how she would break the news to her parents, Charlotte decided that she would leave that until she had completed her shift and had done all that she thought necessary for Mr. Chambers's treatment.

As the moments to the end of her shift passed, Charlotte heard many voices in her head, and not all were good. But then she recalled a Scripture that said something like, "Do not take revenge – vengeance is mine says the Lord."

And she heard another voice in her head saying, "You're a doctor, Charlotte. You are not God. Not God. Not God."

Charlotte knew the voice was that of her grandmother. The voice continued, "Do the right thing, always do the right thing, Precious." That was the name her mother called her as a young child, but she was sure the voice in her head was the voice of her grandmother.

During the weeks Alex Chambers lay drifting in and out of consciousness, Charlotte struggled with the thought of how easy it would be for her to take her revenge on Alex for the pain and suffering his abuse of her mother had caused. It was during such times voices in her head told her she could either help Alex survive or she could prolong his suffering. She struggled to remember the Hippocratic Oath she had taken on becoming a medical doctor. But most of all it was the voice of her grandmother, Ma Beckles, that she heard telling her to always do the right thing.

Charlotte wrestled with the thought of revealing to Amanda that Alex Chambers was in the hospital and a patient assigned to her care. Charlotte's dilemma with telling her mother was twofold: Would it give her mother satisfaction that Chambers had received what was coming to him for what he had done to her? Would it deepen the wound her mother had suppressed over the years?

Charlotte's relationship with her mother since the night of the revelation of the abuse remained loving but strained. On her off duty days and visits home, her parents would enquire how she was and how things were at the hospital. Charlotte's responses lacked the enthusiasm they had before. Charlotte kept up her interaction with her brothers, giving them treats and days out where possible. But her relationship and interaction with her parents was lacklustre. Neither Charlotte nor her mother or her stepfather were able to raise the subject of the abuse. Where in the past Charlotte felt free to share news in her letters from Marcia, she no longer felt able to do so even when the letters from Marcia were funny. She did, however, always pass on greetings from Aunt Maisie and Charlie.

As Charlotte returned to duty following her days off, her first priority was an update on her caseloads and critical care patients. To her surprise, she was informed that Mr. Chambers had made significant improvement and his consciousness was stable. As she proceeded with the consultant and ward staff on the ward round, she reached his bed and found the patient sitting up, free of the many tubes she had last seen him with.

Upon reaching Alex Chambers' bed, Charlotte offered the usual doctor-patient greetings: "Good morning, Mr. Chambers, so good ... " but before Charlotte could complete her greeting, Chambers replied, "Good morning, Dr. Amanda." Her heart skipped a beat, but Charlotte showed him her name badge and replied, "Sorry, sir, I'm Dr. Charlotte Beckles, I've been looking after you."

Alex replied, "Sorry, Doctor, but you look so much like someone I knew back home who was named Amanda."

Charlotte completed her rounds, anxious to

put some distance between herself and this patient and hoping his return to consciousness would not lead to another incident of him confusing her with her mother. Why was he here? Was this just a bizarre coincidence or was he here to confront the need for long overdue discussions? Charlotte wondered if the time was right to share with her parents that Alex was here, of all places.

At the end of her shift, Charlotte returned to her room and kicked off her shoes, throwing her stethoscope on the bed. Then she knelt by the side of her bed as she poured out her heart to God amidst an abundance of tears. She remembered her beloved grandmother as she prayed to God for courage, guidance, and inspiration. As Charlotte prayed for guidance and the wisdom to deal with the days ahead with Alex Chambers regaining consciousness, she wondered how she was going to tell her family she had been caring for him for weeks. She considered asking to be released from her assignment to his care but what excuse could she give? How could she explain that it was a conflict of interest and what that conflict was?

During the weeks she had been attending to Alex, she would often look at him, knowing what he had done to her mother and wonder, "How could the genes of such a person be part of her? How could she ever consider him to be anything other than a monster, a villain—never her father." As these thoughts ran through her mind, it came to her that having the blood and genes of Alex Chambers did not make him her father.

She wondered too what it was really like for her own mother when she looked at Charlotte. Just as she had been looking at Chambers, was

Charlotte a reminder to her mother of the dreadful day she was abused by him? It pained Charlotte as these thoughts ran through her head, thinking of the weight her mother must have carried at the memory of the abuse, the pregnancy, the estrangement and her clashes with Aunt Maisie.

Although her mother seemed happy now, Charlotte wondered, *Was she really free? Can one really ever be free from trauma?* Charlotte could only imagine that her mother's strength and resilience had come from the love and support she received from beloved Ma Beckles, the support of her mother Evelyn, and now being blessed with a loving husband, sons, and the faith in God she seemed to embrace.

As Charlotte poured out her heart to God, overwhelmed by uncontrollable tears, she prayed for the wisdom and strength to tell her parents that the man who had abused her mother and had caused so much suffering in her family was only a few miles away. Despite agonising over the thought that such a revelation might once again resurface in her mother's mind the memories of the abuse and the separation from her parents, she came to the conclusion that the best thing to do was to tell her parents. Hopefully it would finally put the ghost of the past to rest.

Charlotte felt sure that the strength her mother had shown all these years would now enable her to deal with the knowledge that Alex Chambers was so nearby. At best, she could expect that her mother would only be curious as to why he was in the UK and so close by—it being such coincidence that he ended up at the hospital where Charlotte was working and him being one of her patients. Charlotte smiled to herself as she imagined that her beloved Grandma Beckles would say it was the hand of God to which her parents would probably agree.

Now that she had finally made up her mind to visit her parents with the news, she climbed into bed. Turning out the lights, thoughts of Marcia and the family she had grown up with came to her mind. She especially thought of the many hours and conversations she and Marcia shared as they turned out the light when they went to bed. How many years had passed and so many changes taken placed. Marcia had rekindled her relationship with Brian; Charlie and his girlfriend now had a baby girl they had named Charlotte; Yvonne was now at university; and with the passing of her husband, Aunt Maisie had become a practising Christian.

Over the years since Charlotte had been in England, the previously strained relationship between her and her aunt had developed into one of love and respect. Recalling her conversations with her aunt as a child brought to mind the sharpness of Aunt Maisie's tongue. During those times she would remember her grandmother and at the times she had sometimes wished it was Aunt Maise who had passed away instead of Ma Beckles.

With such thoughts running through her head, she made the sign of the cross on her chest just as she had often done as a child. This was a common practice amongst children on the Island when they told lies or said or did things they knew grownups would not approve of, as they were often told by adults that God would punish them if they did not make the sign of the cross and say, "God forgive me." The thought of this made

Charlotte smile as she settled herself down into bed. The matter was settled she would visit her parents first thing in the morning.

The next morning, Charlotte hummed a tune as she prepared to make her visit to her parents. She no longer felt the need to recite what she was going to say to them. She felt comfortable with her decision to inform her parents that Alex was only a few miles away. Clear in her mind that it was the right thing to do, she set off to the visit to her parents.

Getting into her car and turning on the radio, she herd the iconic voice of Bob Marley singing *Redemption Song*. She joined in with the song, singing at the top of her voice as if to drown out any intervening thoughts that would put her off her mission. Charlotte came to the conclusion that Alex's near-death experience and her meeting him as she did was not just a coincidence. Somehow there was a greater purpose behind it all. Charlotte felt that in many ways their meeting was meant to be. She wondered what her beloved grandmother Ma Beckles would make of it.

The closer Charlotte got to her parents' home, the more sure she was that her mother would be okay. The life that her mother now lived, and what her mother had received through her faith in God, was greater than what Alex Chambers had taken from her—and nothing and no one would take that away. Charlotte felt sure that her mother's response to the news would be to pray for Alex and to forgive him completely— which is exactly what she had decided to. After all, her grandmother had told her to always do the right thing.

THE END

ABOUT GLORIA OKOSI

Gloria Okosi was born and raised on the island of Barbados. Growing up in a small island, she recalls life in her neighbourhood being quiet and routine, except for the sounds of children playing outdoors during their past times.

Gloria migrated to the United Kingdom in the 1960s, at a time when many people were leaving the islands of the Caribbean either to study or to find employment in Britain as skilled or unskilled workers. Arriving in a big, bustling city in the UK was a big change from home, and very daunting.

Having had a desire for a career in the caring professions since childhood, when the opportunity to study nursing in the UK arose Gloria took it, beginning her career in 1966. This was in the era of the "Swinging 60s", a time when Britain was a melting pot of different nationalities, cultures, fashions and music, and the period of "flower power," the Hare Krishna movement, racial tension, the start of The Troubles in Northern Ireland, and the Black Power movement in the US. Amidst this time of change, Gloria's Christian faith and upbringing helped to keep her focused on achieving her goal of becoming a nurse — the reason she left her island home. Following qualification, Gloria spent most of her working life as a nurse, later transferring her skills to social work. It was her knowledge and experience of these professions that helped fashion the main characters in *Charlotte's Story*.

The opening scenes of the book were inspired by Gloria's memories of listening to the dulcet tones of Richard Benaud's radio commentary on a cricket match between Australia and the West Indies many years ago. As he beautifully described the surroundings of Barbados' Kensington Oval cricket ground, with trees blowing in the wind and egrets feeding on ticks as they sat on the backs of the cows, Gloria was transported back to her childhood growing up on the island.